P9-ARN-164

LONE STAR HEROINES

SECRETS
in the
SKY

Melinda Rice

Illustrations by Toni Thomas

Other books in the Lone Star Heroines series:

Fire on the Hillside
by Melinda Rice

Messenger on the Battlefield
by Melinda Rice

The Lone Star Heroes series:

Comanche Peace Pipe
by Patrick Dearen

On the Pecos Trail
by Patrick Dearen

The Hidden Treasure of the Chisos
by Patrick Dearen

LONE STAR HEROINES

SECRETS
in the
SKY

Melinda Rice

Republic of Texas Press
Plano, Texas

Library of Congress Cataloging-in-Publication Data

Rice, Melinda.
   Secrets in the sky / Melinda Rice.
      p. cm. — (Lone Star heroines)
   Summary: While her brother is off flying planes for the Air Corps,
twelve-year-old Bethany becomes involved with women training with
the Women Airforce Service Pilots (WASPs) right in her hometown of
Sweetwater, Texas.
   ISBN 1-55622-787-6 (pbk.)
   1. World War, 1939-1945—Texas—Sweetwater—Juvenile fiction.
[1. World War, 1939-1945—Texas—Sweetwater—Fiction. 2. Women
Airforce Service Pilots (U.S.)—Fiction. 3. Texas—Fiction.] I. Title.

PZ7.R3647 Se 2001
[Fic]—dc21   00-068966
                              CIP

© 2001, Melinda Rice
All Rights Reserved

Republic of Texas Press is an imprint of Wordware Publishing, Inc.
No part of this book may be reproduced in any form or by
any means without permission in writing from
Wordware Publishing, Inc.

Printed in the United States of America

ISBN 1-55622-787-6
10 9 8 7 6 5 4 3 2 1
0101

All inquiries for volume purchases of this book should be addressed to
Wordware Publishing, Inc., at 2320 Los Rios Boulevard, Plano, Texas 75074.
Telephone inquiries may be made by calling:
(972) 423-0090

1

February 1943
Sweetwater, Texas

Bethany Parker swiped at the tears on her cheeks. She'd lost her handkerchief, as usual, so she sniffed hard. She didn't mind using her hands to dab her eyes and face, but there was no way she was going to use them to wipe her nose.

She sniffed again.

"How could she just leave like that?" Bethany wondered out loud.

"She had to go. It was what she had to do to help win the war," said Mags, handing over a spare hanky.

Margaret Wells was Bethany's best friend. No one but her grandmother called her Margaret, and Mags wouldn't answer to it if anyone else tried. It was Mags or Maggie, or you could consider yourself ignored.

Bethany—who didn't like nicknames, especially "Beth" because she thought it sounded like a cat coughing up a hairball—smiled her thanks. Mags always carried an extra handkerchief just for her.

"No, Mags. There had to be another way. She didn't have to leave."

Mags sighed. Bethany knew her friend was tired of this conversation. They'd been talking about the movie all week.

The two girls buttoned up their coats as they pushed opened the door of the movie theater and stepped out onto the sidewalk. They had just seen *Casablanca* for the second time. Even though they had known what was going to happen, they still cried when Ingrid Bergman got on the plane and left Humphrey Bogart.

Maggie would have gotten on the plane.

Bethany would have stayed with Humphrey Bogart.

But it was too cold to stand around talking about it any more. Bethany's father always said there were two seasons in Sweetwater—hot and cold. And right now, it was cold. Very, very cold.

Snow lay in dirty heaps on both sides of Main Street, and the wind whistled between the buildings and down the girls' collars, making them shiver.

Mags turned right, headed for home, and Bethany turned left. She and Mags lived only a block and a half apart, but Bethany never went straight home anymore. She always stopped at the post office first.

There might be a letter from Andrew.

So far, her brother had written every week since he'd been gone—just a little more than a year now. He had joined the Army right after the Japanese bombed Pearl Harbor and was gone by Christmas. Now they had spent two Christmases without Andrew, and Bethany missed him terribly. He was flying planes for the Air Corps and she was proud of him. But she missed him.

It seemed she missed him more all the time. Mamma said that not knowing when they would see him again (she never said "if") made it worse. But whenever Mamma said that, Papa always said, "Sure we know when we'll see him again—when we win the war."

But nobody knew when that would be.

Folks talked about it all the time. Sometimes it seemed like the only thing anyone *ever* talked about anymore—at the café and after church, at Papa's barbershop, at the post office. Even on the radio and in the movies, it was war, war, war. *Casablanca* was about the war. Thinking about that made Bethany sniff again.

Mags was wrong. There just *had* to be a way for Ingrid Bergman to help win the war *and* stay with Humphrey Bogart.

Bethany hurried on down the street, her head bent into the wind and her hand clutching her collar tight. The cold could not get at her neck, but it did whoosh up her skirt.

One of these days, she thought, I am going to wear pants to school no matter what Mamma thinks, and Mamma can just go ahead and have that conniption fit. Come to think of it, Bethany wasn't sure just exactly what a conniption fit was. If Mamma had one, what would happen? Would she foam at the mouth? Would she turn purple with green spots? I guess I could just ask Mamma, Bethany thought. But somehow, that did not seem like a good idea.

When Bethany finally reached the post office, her teeth were chattering. The walk couldn't have taken more than ten minutes, but the temperature made it seem three times that long. She was so eager to get out of the wind that she flung the door open harder than she intended. It banged back on its hinges, and a great gust of icy air followed her into the building.

That earned her a frown from Mrs. Petrie, who had just picked up a package. Mrs. Petrie was always frowning about something, though. Bethany just closed the door, smiled sweetly, and headed to the counter.

Mr. Robinson, the postmaster, was waiting for her.

"Letter from Andrew, Bethany. Be sure to give him our best." He handed over the letter.

"Thanks, Mr. Robinson. We'll tell him," she said.

"You know, Bethany, we do deliver the mail. You don't have to come in here every day," Mr. Robinson told her.

Bethany nodded. She knew.

But she didn't want to wait. She wanted to get the letter as soon as it arrived. Checking for mail at the post office also gave her an excuse not to go straight home from school every day, and *that* increased her chances of catching an afternoon movie with Mags. Bethany loved the movies.

She slipped the letter into her coat pocket and then remembered that was the pocket where her handkerchief had been—and she had lost the handkerchief. Better not put the letter there, she thought. Instead, she unbuttoned her coat and put the letter in her skirt pocket. That should keep it safe.

Buttoning up again, she smiled at Mrs. Petrie, who was talking with Mrs. Collins. Probably complaining about ill-mannered young women, Bethany thought grumpily. No, she decided, they were most likely talking about the war. Mrs. Petrie's sons, all three of them, were in the Army, and Mrs. Collins's oldest son had just joined the Navy.

Bethany left the post office and hurried back the way she had come. With the wind at her back, it didn't seem quite so cold. Three more blocks and she'd turn right on Maple Street.

Bethany never had understood why it was called Maple Street; there were no maple trees on it. There were no maple trees in all of Sweetwater or the whole of Nolan County, as far as she could tell.

Whenever she brought it up, though, Mamma said she'd be better off spending the time thinking about her geometry (or whichever subject she was having trouble with in school that year; this year it was geometry).

But Mamma never answered the question about the maple trees. So far, no one ever had.

Maple Street was where Papa's barbershop was, though, so that's where she was headed. Bethany told herself she wanted to stop and tell Papa about the letter from Andrew, but she knew she was really hoping for a ride home.

She was almost there, to Maple Street, when a movement on the other side of Main Street caught her eye. It was a woman getting out of a taxi at the Bluebonnet Hotel.

Oh my gosh, it's Ingrid Bergman! thought Bethany. The movie she had just seen was still fresh in her mind.

A longer look convinced her the woman was not the gorgeous star of *Casablanca*. But who could she be? No one in Sweetwater looked like that.

The woman had on a raccoon coat. At least, Bethany *thought* it was a raccoon coat. She had never actually seen one up close. And, was that *slacks* that the woman was wearing? It was! Mamma would have a conniption. An image of her mother foaming at the mouth popped into Bethany's mind, and she shook her head to get rid of the vision.

By now the woman had disappeared inside the hotel. Who was she? Bethany just *had* to know.

She crossed the street and ran into the hotel—and smacked right into the woman from the taxi. No wait, it was a different woman—slim and elegant like the other, but dark-haired. The woman outside had been blondish.

As Bethany looked around for the woman she had first seen, she realized the hotel lobby was full of women who had that same look, that look of not being from Sweetwater. There must be at least two dozen of them! What was going on?!

All of a sudden, she remembered the woman she had bumped when she ran into the hotel. The woman was crouched on the floor, gathering the scattered contents of her purse. Bethany dropped down beside her and picked up a tube of lipstick.

"Hi. I'm sorry I ran into you," she said, handing over the lipstick. It was Ravenous Red. Nobody in Sweetwater wore Ravenous Red lipstick.

"What are you?" Bethany blurted, then blushed. She figured her face must have turned redder than the lipstick she had just returned. She had meant to say, "*Who* are you?"

But the woman did not take offence. She just laughed and said, "Why I'm Josephine Nicholson from California, and I'm a pilot. Who and what are you?"

"I'm Bethany Parker and I'm twelve and I live here in Sweetwater and are you really a pilot? My brother's a pilot." Bethany's words just tumbled out. The woman was a pilot like Andrew!

"Hello, Bethany. Nice to meet you," said Josephine Nicholson from California. She snapped her purse shut and stood up. "Yes, I am a pilot. We're all pilots," she said, gesturing around the room with a graceful sweep of her arm. "We're here to fly for the war."

Bethany did not know what to say. Women flying for the war? Flying like Andrew? Flying in Sweetwater?

"You mean you're going to go and drop bombs on the Germans?" she asked. That's what Andrew did.

"No," said Josephine Nicholson from California. "We're going to fly the planes here at home so the men can go fight overseas. But first, we've got to learn to fly the Army way."

What did that mean? Bethany started to ask, but the pilot interrupted her.

"Look," the pilot continued. "I've got to get settled here, but we'll be staying at the hotel for a while until they make room for us out at the base. Why don't you come back and visit me tomorrow?"

"Really?" asked Bethany.

"Really. Drop by tomorrow after school."

"Can I bring a friend?" asked Bethany, thinking of Mags.

"Absolutely."

2

"**P**apa, guess what! You'll never guess! There are women pilots at the Bluebonnet Hotel. They're going to fly for the war!" cried Bethany, bursting into her father's barbershop on Maple Street.

She had forgotten all about the maple trees and the lack of them in Sweetwater.

Instead, her mind was filled with images of elegant women in the open cockpits of airplanes, their hair fluttering in the wind as they swooped and zoomed in the air over her hometown.

She imagined she was one of them, with a flowing white scarf around her neck like the pilots in the movies always wore. Her plane would be a lovely purple, she decided. If there could be a Red Baron, why not a Purple Baroness? Bethany saw herself in the cockpit. As she flew, she peered ahead through the clouds. Finally, she spotted her prey. It was the Red Baron! She swooped down on him, firing her machine gun as she went.

Rat-a-tat-tat-tat-tat-tat-tat! Rat-a-tat-tat-tat-tat-tat-tat-tat! Rat-a-tat-tat-tat-tat-tat-tat!

He was hit! As his plane plunged downward, the Red Baron looked up at Bethany and saluted. He knew he had been beaten by the best. Bethany, the Purple Baroness, had saved the day.

As she returned his salute, Bethany remembered that she was *not* flying an airplane. She was *not* the Purple Baroness.

No, she was standing in her father's barbershop, and she had just saluted Papa, Mr. McBeath who was getting his hair cut, and three other men sitting in the shop. There were always people in the barbershop, even if no one wanted a haircut. They sat around and talked—mostly about the war these days.

For the second time that afternoon, Bethany blushed. Ravenous Red, she thought, as the men chuckled. Bethany hated being laughed at. She was glad they didn't know about the Purple Baroness.

"Well, Parker, it looks like the war really is coming to the home front now," Mr. Baines said to her father. "Does your wife salute you, too? Or is it only your daughter?"

The men, including her father, laughed again. Bethany *really* hated being laughed at. She closed her eyes and imagined it was Mr. Baines in the plane she had shot down.

"So, Bethany, how do you happen to know about the women pilots?" Papa asked. "They just got here."

She explained, leaving out the part about how she first thought one of the women was Ingrid Bergman *and* the part about making Josephine Nicholson from California spill her purse. She'd been laughed at quite enough for one day, thank you.

Bethany also decided not to mention the fact that she was going back to the hotel to visit the pilots tomorrow. If no one knew, she reasoned, no one could tell her not to go.

"I'll tell you what," Mr. Baines was saying. "We're in for a world of trouble now. Those women will be crashing left and right, you wait and see. I bet they'll be knockin' down the telegraph wires and landin' on the courthouse square. No one will be safe."

Mr. McBeath shook his head. The sudden movement made Bethany's father nick the man's ear with his barber scissors.

"My fault, Parker. Sorry," Mr. McBeath said.

While Bethany's father got a plaster for the cut, Mr. McBeath turned in the barber chair so he could keep talking to Mr. Baines.

"Now what makes you say that?" he asked. "All those women are qualified pilots. They're just coming here for a little extra training. It won't be any different than what we're already used to."

Pilots had been coming to Sweetwater to learn to "fly the Army way" for almost a year. But until now, all the pilots had been male.

Last year the town council had leased the city airport to the War Department for just one dollar. Papa had said it was the town's patriotic duty. The War Department needed a place to train pilots, and whoever was in charge thought Sweetwater was the perfect place. Bethany always wondered why. It's not that she didn't like her hometown, but pilots were glamorous and Sweetwater *definitely* was not, she thought.

She remembered that Mr. McBeath's newspaper, the *Sweetwater Reporter*, wrote all about it, then sponsored a contest to give the airfield a new name. Nice old Mr. Pettigrew had suggested Avenger Field. With the terrible bombing at Pearl Harbor still so fresh in everybody's minds, his entry was declared the winner. People wanted to avenge all those deaths. Bethany's mother had said she thought the name was too bloodthirsty. But most everyone else liked it. Bethany liked it.

Since the renaming, lots of pilots had come to Sweetwater. Some came all the way from Canada. Some even came from England. Bethany liked the way the English pilots talked—just like Errol Flynn in the movies. She saw the English pilots in town sometimes, at the movies or shopping at Levy's Department Store.

Andrew was in England now. He lived there and flew a plane that dropped bombs on those stupid Nazis. Bethany wondered if

Andrew would sound like the English pilots when he came home.

If he came home.

Bethany never said "if" in front of Mamma. But she always thought it.

She wondered what Andrew would think of these women pilots.

They had seen a woman pilot once before, a long time ago, before the war. Bethany had been eight. The woman looped the loop in an enormous biplane out at the airport, the one that got renamed Avenger Field.

Bethany remembered that Andrew had paid fifty cents for a ride in the plane, and Bethany had begged for a ride, too. But Mamma and Papa said she was too small.

Bethany grinned. That was before I was the Purple Baroness, she thought. But she didn't say anything.

Mr. Baines was still arguing with Mr. McBeath.

"Now look here, women just don't belong in the cockpit of an airplane," Mr. Baines said. "They don't have the right temperament for it. If it was up to me, this foolishness would never be allowed."

Papa held Mr. McBeath's head still so he couldn't shake it again. The newspaperman kept arguing, though.

"These women already have their pilot's licenses. They're here to learn precision flying for the Civilian Air Corps. They're experienced flyers," he said. "How could that be true if they didn't have the right temperament for it?"

Before Mr. Baines could answer, Mr. Morris, who was sitting next to Mr. Baines and listening to the discussion, jumped in.

"If the government didn't think they were qualified, they wouldn't have sent them here," he said. "Women work in the factories now and you don't have a problem with that. Baines, your own daughter works in a factory up north. Having women fly planes is no different than having them work in factories. There's a war on man. Everyone has to do his part."

Mr. Baines scowled and got up from his chair.

"It *is* different and it ought to be stopped," he said. "My daughter helps build airplanes. She doesn't fly them. She stays on the ground where she belongs."

With that, he jammed his hat on his head, put on his coat, and left the barbershop.

Bethany took his seat against the wall under a big poster of a rattlesnake. The snake was coiled and poised to strike. Blood dripped from its fangs. It looked awfully menacing. In big black letters the poster declared, LESS DANGEROUS THAN CARELESS TALK.

There were posters like that all over town. Bethany liked the one in the post office that showed a battleship on fire and sinking. It said LOOSE LIPS MIGHT SINK SHIPS. She thought that was clever. But Papa liked the rattlesnake poster best. That's why he had it in his shop. He said it was appropriate for Sweetwater because of all the snakes that lived here. "Sweetwater is the rattle-snake capital of the world!" Papa would say.

Bethany didn't know if she believed that. Papa was always teasing about something, after all. But there certainly were a great many rattlesnakes around. How could anyone know where the snake capital was, though? And what would it be capital *of?* The United States of Snakedom? Bethany grinned at the thought. She'd have to remember to tell that one to Papa later. He'd think it was funny.

The men in the shop had stopped talking about the women pilots. In fact, they'd stopped talking about anything at all. So Bethany took the opportunity to ask a question. It was something she'd wondered about ever since the snake poster and the others went up in town.

"Papa," she said, eyeing the poster. "Why does it matter what we say in Sweetwater? The war is far away and there are no spies around here."

"Oh? And just how do you know that, my girl? Spies don't go around advertising that they're spies. They don't wear signs," he said. "In a war, you never know what kind of information will help the enemy. That's why it's important to watch what you say and who you say it to."

Bethany had never thought about it that way, but she couldn't imagine what she could have to say that would help a spy. Besides, spies were glamorous. They were always smuggling secret documents and sabotaging things. There was nothing to smuggle in Sweetwater, nothing to blow up. Spies were glamorous. Sweetwater was not. Of course, pilots were glamorous, too, and there were plenty of pilots in Sweetwater these days.

But that was different.

3

Bethany had been so excited about meeting Josephine Nicholson from California that she forgot all about the letter from Andrew. She didn't remember it until she took off her coat after she and Papa got home.

"Oh Mamma, Papa. There's a new letter from Andrew!" she said.

Bethany pulled the letter from the pocket of her blue wool skirt and handed it to her mother. Mamma smiled.

"We'll save it for dessert," she said. Then, like always, she propped the letter against the picture of Andrew on the mantle over the fireplace in the living room. The Parker family had a ritual for reading Andrew's letters.

First, Mamma put the letter by the photograph on the mantle. The picture had been taken right after Andrew finished pilot training and earned his wings, right before he shipped out to England. He was smiling, and he looked so handsome in his uniform. He had blue eyes and straight, light brown hair—just like Bethany. But you couldn't tell that from the photo.

Next, the Parkers ate supper. Tonight it was pinto beans, rice, corn bread, and spinach. Bethany was developing a real hatred of pinto beans. They ate them with rice for supper at least once a week, and Bethany was thoroughly sick of them.

"I wonder how much is crossed out this time," she said, pushing beans around on her plate.

Sometimes there were so many words blacked out in Andrew's letters that there was hardly anything left to read. When that happened, the Parkers were all disappointed.

The military people went over all the soldiers' letters before they got mailed and crossed out anything they felt might help the enemy if the enemy happened to intercept the letters.

More spy stuff, thought Bethany. LOOSE LIPS MIGHT SINK SHIPS.

She wondered who might intercept Andrew's letters. Mr. Robinson at the post office?

Bethany conjured up an image of the postmaster. He was thin and tall, much taller than Papa. He was so tall that when he talked to you he was usually peering down at you over the tops of his little wire-rimmed glasses. Those glasses perched on a pointy nose, and they were always smudged. Mr. Robinson had a big ole' Adam's apple that bobbed up and down when he talked. He was very kind. And lately, he'd been very sad. He and his wife had gotten one of *those* telegrams last summer. Their son, Bobby, had been killed during the Battle of Midway.

No, Bethany couldn't see Mr. Robinson as a spy.

"Bethany, the sooner you quit playing with those beans and eat them, the sooner we can have dessert," said Mamma. She meant Andrew's letter. As soon as they finished eating, they would all go into the living room and read it together.

"Sorry, Mamma," said Bethany between quick bites of beans and rice. "I was just thinking."

As she hurried through the rest of her meal, Papa told Mamma about the women pilots.

"It's a women's flying detachment named after some kind of bug," he said. "The Bees or the Hornets or something. I hear they're going to assign the women to ferry planes stateside to free up more men for combat."

Bethany couldn't help herself. She interrupted. "Mamma, Mr. Baines says women don't have the right temperament to fly planes. He says they're all going to crash. Do you think that's true?"

Bethany's mother thought about it for a minute. "Well, I suppose some have the right temperament for it and some don't," she said. "Now finish your supper."

4

The Parkers weren't disappointed this time. The military censors had crossed out very little in Andrew's letter.

Dear Mamma, Papa and Bethany,

Thanks for the dandy care package. The socks and the candy bars were especially appreciated. Mamma, I am sorry to say your cookies did not survive the journey too well, but we ate the crumbs and they tasted just fine to us. I shared the goodies with the crew. As I've told you before, they're a fine bunch of fellows. I'm proud to fly with them.

The socks I kept for myself. It gets cold in the plane when we XXXXXXXXXXXXXXXXXXXXXXXXXXXXX XXX XXXXXXXXXXXXXXXXXXXXXXXXXXXXXX XXXXXXXXXXXXXXXXXXXXXXXXXXXXXXXXXX XXXXXXXXXX. It certainly lives up to its nickname. It really is a Flying Fortress. And that's just fine with us!!! It seems a strange way to fight a war. We XXXXXXX XXXXXXXXXXX and XXXXXXXXXXXXXXXX XXXXXXXXXXXXXXXX then return to base. It's almost like Papa going to and from work at the barbershop back home. But I don't issue the orders, I just obey them.

It's cold on the ground here, too, but not as cold as it gets in Sweetwater this time of year. The English people are very nice. They have suffered terribly and there seem to be shortages of everything, but they always seem happy to share what they have. Remember, they have been at war much longer than we have. I don't know how they manage it, but they do not seem down in the dumps on the whole. While not exactly what you might call cheerful, they are certainly determined. They call it "having a stiff upper lip" and they have no thought of anything but winning the war. Three cheers for them!

Bethany, how are you doing with your geometry? I wish I was there to help you with your homework. Stick with it. I know you'll get it. I miss you all terribly and remember you every night in my prayers. Remember me in yours.

Love,

Your Son and Brother

Andrew

Mamma folded up the letter and tucked it into the pocket of her dress. She would put it with all the others. Sometimes Bethany found her with a whole stack of Andrew's letters, reading them all again, one by one. She must have some of them memorized by now.

Nobody said anything. They never did after reading a letter from Andrew. Mamma went into the kitchen to wash up the supper dishes. Bethany went to her room to do her homework (more of the dreaded geometry!) and Papa settled down in his chair by the fireplace to read the *Sweetwater Reporter.*

The next day, Bethany couldn't wait until school was over. She was going to talk to Josephine Nicholson from California. She begged Mags to go with her, but Mags had to work in her father's store that afternoon. Mr. Wells was the town druggist. Mags helped out when he was short-handed. She swept up and restocked the shelves and sometimes worked behind the soda counter.

"Come by after you talk with the lady pilots. Papa will let us have a hot chocolate," said Mags. Bethany promised she would.

She was so excited that her stomach did little flip-flops as she walked to the Bluebonnet Hotel. She didn't notice the cold at all. When she got there, she looked around the lobby eagerly. She saw several women she was sure must be pilots, but Josephine Nicholson from California was not among them.

She asked at the front desk. The clerk told her Miss Nicholson was in room 502. By the time she had climbed five flights of stairs, Bethany had a stitch in her side. She found room 502, then stood there staring at the number on the door. What if Josephine Nicholson from California had changed her mind? What if she didn't really want to talk with a girl from Sweetwater who always lost her handkerchiefs and couldn't do geometry problems?

Bethany could hear laughter from inside the room. Taking a few deep breaths to calm herself, she raised her hand and timidly knocked on the door. Tap, tap, tap. The laughter inside continued, and nobody answered. Somebody on the other side of the door started singing.

Bethany knew the song. It was played all the time on the Lucky Strike Hit Parade show on the radio.

Taking a deep breath, she knocked again, louder this time. The door swung open. Bethany looked up expectantly. A tall woman in a bathrobe stood there. A smattering of freckles marched across her pale face from one cheek, up over her nose to the other cheek. Her hair was covered by a towel, wrapped like a turban around her head. Bethany would have bet anything that the hair under it was red.

"Hi," said the woman. Bethany realized she was staring. She felt stupid just standing there not saying anything.

"Hi," she said. "Is Josephine Nicholson here?"

"Sure. Just a minute," said the woman. As she turned away, she pulled the towel off her head and Bethany saw that she was indeed a redhead. "Jo! Visitor for you," said the redhead.

The singing had stopped.

Then Josephine Nicholson was at the door. She was even more beautiful than Bethany had remembered. Her shoulder-length hair was a dark, dark brown, almost but not quite black. Her eyes were brown, too, but much lighter, more like caramel. When the pilot saw who it was at the door, she smiled, revealing two even rows of pretty white teeth.

"Hi, Bethany! Come on in. I'm glad you're here," said the gorgeous creature. Bethany was relieved. She silently obeyed, and Josephine Nicholson shut the door behind her.

There was another woman in the room, but it wasn't the one who had opened the door. The redhead had disappeared through another doorway. Probably the bathroom, Bethany decided.

"Bethany, this is Lynn Strickland," said Josephine Nicholson, pointing to the other woman, who smiled and nodded at Bethany from where she sat in a chair by the window. She had brown hair too, darker than Bethany's but not as dark as Josephine's. Her eyes were hazel.

"Hi," said Bethany. All of a sudden, she felt very shy and formal so she started using her company manners. "Miss Nicholson," she said. "Thank you for letting me come see you. I really am very sorry about running into you yesterday."

"Call me Jo," said the pilot, as she flung herself down on one of the room's two beds. "Don't you waste another thought on yesterday. I'm glad you came. Come sit down and tell me about yourself."

"Golly, there's not much to tell. I'm twelve and I've lived in Sweetwater all my life," said Bethany. She perched on the side of the other bed and wracked her brain trying to think of something interesting to say to Jo. She said the name to herself again. Jo...Jo, Jo, Jo, Jo, Jo. Like her favorite character in *Little Women*. She decided she liked it. But she still couldn't think of anything to say that might be even remotely interesting to her new friend. The fact that she hated geometry really didn't seem to qualify.

"Didn't you tell me yesterday that your brother is a pilot?" Jo asked.

Of course! She could talk about Andrew! That would be interesting. So she told Jo and Lynn all about how Andrew flew a B-17 bomber out of England and how he said it was so damp there all the time. And she told them with pride how he had named his plane the Brave Bethany after her. Just thinking about *that* made her smile. Then she told them about the care packages they sent her brother. She told them how much she missed him.

But Bethany was tired of talking about herself. She wanted to know more about these women who were going to fly airplanes for the war effort—these women who weren't from Sweetwater.

"My father says your group is named after a bug, but he couldn't remember which one," she said.

Jo and Lynn looked startled.

"Well, we flygirls have been called a lot of things, but never a bug. At least not until now," said Lynn. "That is definitely a new one."

Then Jo started chuckling. "Lynn, I'll bet he meant wasp."

She spelled it out. "W-A-S-P!" Both women were silent for a second, then howled with laughter. Jo laughed so hard that she wrapped her arms around her ribcage and rolled right off the bed onto the floor. Thud! Bethany didn't see what was so funny.

Seeing her confusion, Jo sat up and explained that she and Lynn were part of an organization called the Women Airforce Service Pilots. W.A.S.P. for short. WASP, not wasp. Then Bethany understood, and she giggled too.

"How about this for our motto—'The WASP: Our bite is worse than our buzz!'" cried Lynn.

Bethany and the pilots laughed again. This time they laughed together.

They continued to snicker as the redheaded girl came out of the bathroom. She was dressed now in slacks and a long-sleeved blouse.

"Bethany, meet Carla Neely. Carla, this is our new pal Bethany," said Jo.

Bethany beamed. *Their new pal.* She was one of the gang! At that moment, she decided she, too, would become a pilot one day.

She wondered how a girl would go about that. Andrew had learned to fly in the Army Air Corps, but yesterday Mr. McBeath had said all the women pilots coming to Sweetwater already knew how to fly.

Only one way to find out, she reasoned. So she asked her new pals. As it turned out, they all had different stories. None of them had known any of the others before they were accepted into the WASP. They met in Sweetwater, the same day that Bethany had met Jo.

JO'S STORY:

At twenty-nine, Josephine Nicholson was oldest of the three women sharing room 502 at the Bluebonnet Hotel in Sweetwater. She had also come the furthest to fly with the WASP, all the way from San Francisco, California.

She had wanted to fly airplanes almost her entire life, and she could remember the moment that sparked that desire as clearly as if it had happened an hour ago. She was five years old and she had gone to see a flying exhibition with her father. It was thrilling! Just telling the story to Bethany and the others made her smile, even after all these years.

As Jo and her father watched, the pilot performed loops and spins and rolls that made the crowd gasp, Jo included. Just when it looked like the big bi-plane would surely crash, it would level off, then soar back into the blue, blue sky with a little wiggle of its wings. Every time that happened, Jo was certain it was a message meant just for her. This is fun, the pilot seemed to be telling her. Don't you wish you were up here with me? Jo did.

Finally, the plane landed. She was disappointed to see the beautiful machine stuck on the ground. It looked clumsy and awkward and made her think of the ducks that made their home on the pond in her backyard. On the ground, chasing after the bread crumbs she tossed to them, they waddled comically. But in the air they were things of beauty.

She was eager to see the man who had made the flying machine do such marvelous stunts. He jumped from the cockpit, and Jo was surprised at how short he was. Then he reached up and pulled off the plaid cap he was wearing, and a great mass of dark curls tumbled out. Jo sucked in her breath. *He* was a *she!* It was a girl who had made the airplane do all those wonderful things! Her father had known but kept it to himself so Jo would be surprised. She was, and she jumped up and down, clapping out her delight.

The flyer was the great Katherine Stinson from San Antonio, Texas. She was the fourth woman in the United States to get a pilot's license and the first person—male or female—to perform a snap roll at the top of a loop. But Jo didn't know any of that then. She knew only that watching the petite beauty fly had been the most thrilling experience of her short life. From that moment on, she had wanted to fly. She had been determined.

Jo had no brothers or sisters. Her mother died of fever when she was still a toddler, and her father never remarried. He was a wealthy banker with a jovial, loving disposition. With no other outlet for his affections, he indulged his only child.

Fifteen years after seeing Katherine Stinson fly, when Jo insisted on learning to fly herself, her father found someone to teach her. When she got her pilot's license, he bought her a plane. By the time the bank failed and her father lost his fortune during the Great Depression, she had enough flying experience to get jobs as a pilot. She was able to support herself and help him, too, until she joined the Women Airforce Service Pilots. Jo had more than 500 hours of flight time to her credit when she heard the government was looking for experienced female pilots to help with the war effort. It was never a question of if, only of when, she would apply.

"So here I am," she said. "Now it's Carla's turn."

CARLA'S STORY:

Carla Neely was born and raised on a farm in North Carolina. "Unlike you, Jo, I was most definitely *not* an only child!" she said. Carla was one of nine children: six boys and three girls. She was born fifth. "We had enough to eat and there was always plenty of work to go around, but that's all we had plenty of," Carla said.

She had an uncle and aunt who lived in Chicago, and when war broke out she moved in with them and took a factory job. "I'm a WASP now, but I was a Rosie Riveter," said Carla. "This is most definitely better!"

It had never crossed her mind to become a pilot herself, to fly the planes she was helping to build. But then she started dating a fellow who was taking flying lessons. She went with him to the airfield a few times and grew impatient with watching from the ground while her boyfriend soared above her. Besides, flying looked like fun and Carla was always ready to have fun. So she and her boyfriend convinced his instructor to give her lessons, too. The teacher agreed, thinking Carla would get bored and stop after a few weeks. "No one was more surprised than he was when I got my license!" said Carla in her soft Southern drawl.

It was Carla's uncle who first heard about the WASP and suggested his niece apply. She was interested but feared she did not have enough time in the air to qualify for the program. "So I scrimped and saved," said Carla. "I pinched pennies until they hollered so I could buy time in a plane. And, as Jo said, here I am!"

Bethany wanted to know what happened to the boyfriend. When she asked, Carla grinned and said, "Why, I turned him into my fiancé!" She said he had been drafted and was supposed to go overseas soon. They would marry when he returned.

Bethany noticed that Carla didn't say "if," either.

Carla turned to Lynn and said, "Well, gal, looks like you're up next!"

LYNN'S STORY:

Lynn smiled. "My story isn't as interesting as Jo's or Carla's!" she said.

Jo shook her head. "We'll be the judge of that," she said. "Now come on, out with it!"

Lynn said she was born and raised in Oklahoma City. Her family was neither wealthy nor poor. She had one brother and one sister, both still in high school. "We're just an average little family from an average little place," she said.

Lynn married her high school sweetheart, a boy name Peter Strickland. Like so many young men in America, he volunteered for the Army after Pearl Harbor was bombed.

"He's fighting in North Africa now. I haven't heard from him in a long time," she said sadly. But she smiled when she added, "But I haven't heard from the Army either, so that's good!"

Bethany knew what she meant. If the Army contacted you, it meant your husband (or son . . . or brother) was dead or missing. Nobody wanted to hear from the Army or the Marines or the Navy. Many people did, though. Bethany shivered, thinking of Andrew. Then she turned her attention back to Lynn, who was saying that she had always been interested in flying, but had never had the chance to try it.

When a local college offered a civilian pilot training program, Lynn applied. She was the only woman in a class of twelve students.

"They weren't exactly welcoming," Lynn said. "But I stuck it out and got my license." She had been working as an airmail pilot when she heard about the WASP.

"So here I am too!"

Bethany was fascinated. By the time Lynn finished her story, Bethany was sprawled on the bed on her stomach with her chin propped in her hands. She wanted to know more. She especially wanted to know what the women would be doing while they were in Sweetwater. But then she looked at the alarm clock on the little stand between the two beds. It was after 6 o'clock! She had been there for three hours! Mags was going to be mad at her for not stopping by the drugstore. She would think Bethany had forgotten and gone straight home. Mamma and Papa were going to be angry, too, not to mention a little worried. She had to go home, and she had to do it now!

5

Bethany was gasping as she ran up the walkway to her own front door. She had run all the way home from the Bluebonnet Hotel after explaining to her new friends why she had to leave so suddenly. They had invited her to return the following day, and she hoped she could, but right now all Bethany could think about was what her parents were going to say when she got home.

The door opened just as she reached it. Bethany stopped, breathing hard in the cold evening air. Her warm breath blossomed into little clouds in front of her face and lingered there for a moment before the wind snatched them away. Bethany thought she must look like a steam engine, standing there puffing in the twilight. It was just as cold now as it had been yesterday, but she had worked up a sweat running home. She wasn't the least bit chilly.

Papa stood there in his hat and coat, his car key in his hand. He looked just as surprised to see Bethany standing there as Bethany had been to see the door magically open as she approached. It turned out that he had been going out to look for her.

"Mary, it's okay!" he called over his shoulder. "Bethany's right here!"

He stepped aside and Bethany stepped past him into the warm house. He shut the door behind them as Mamma rushed out from the kitchen. First she hugged Bethany. Then she scolded her.

"Where on earth have you been?" she cried. "I thought you must have gone to a movie with Maggie. But when I called her house she told me she had been working in the drugstore all afternoon and hadn't seen you either. I have been so worried!"

Mags hadn't told Mamma that Bethany was going to see the women pilots! She was such a good friend! But at this point, it seemed Bethany's only real option was to 'fess up. So that is what she did, emphasizing how nice the women were and explaining that she had been so interested in their stories that she had lost track of time.

When she finished her story, she stood there waiting for Mamma and Papa to react. She just knew they were going to forbid her from ever seeing her WASP friends again. It wasn't fair! She had just gotten to know them! How was she supposed to become a pilot if she couldn't talk to Jo?

But Mamma and Papa surprised her. They did ground her—no movies for a whole week and she had to come straight home after school every day. She couldn't even stop at the post office. But Bethany did get permission to stop—briefly!—at the Bluebonnet Hotel the next day to explain to Jo why she wouldn't be visiting again soon.

When she sat down at the dinner table after washing up, Bethany's parents surprised her again.

"Bethany, your father and I have been talking about these women pilots," her mother said.

Bethany groaned to herself. Oh no! Here it comes, she thought. They're going to tell me I can't go tomorrow after all. They're going to tell me I can't talk with Jo anymore!

"Bethany, are you listening?"

"Yes Mamma," Bethany said with dread.

"When you see your pilot friends tomorrow, why don't you invite them over for dinner next Sunday?"

"Oh Mamma, it's not fair! Don't make me! I have to see them again. I just *have* to!" cried Bethany.

"Bethany, did you hear what I said?" her mother asked. In fact, Bethany had not. She had been so busy worrying about what Mamma *might* be going to say that it took her a few minutes to realize what she actually *had* said.

"Mamma, do you mean it?" she asked. When her mother confirmed that, yes, she had indeed invited Jo and Lynn and Carla to Sunday dinner, Bethany scraped her chair back from the table and hopped up from her seat. She almost knocked her plate of meat loaf and mashed potatoes onto the floor as she rushed around the table to where Mamma sat so she could hug her from behind.

"Oh thank you, thank you! That's just swell! You're the greatest, the absolute greatest!" Bethany said. And she meant it. She couldn't wait to tell Mags! She couldn't wait to tell Jo and Lynn and Carla!

"Yes, well you're welcome," Mamma said, patting her hand. "You just remember that I'm the greatest the next time we have pinto beans for supper!" They all laughed.

6

The next day after school, Mags went with Bethany to issue the invitation to Sunday dinner. Just as Bethany had feared, Maggie had been mad about yesterday. Once Bethany had explained, though, Mags forgave her and everything was okay. On the way to the hotel, Bethany told Mags all about Jo and Lynn and Carla. Mags couldn't wait to meet them.

At the hotel, Bethany quickly cut across the lobby and headed for the stairs with Maggie close behind. When they were halfway across the room, Bethany heard someone calling her name. It was Jo.

Bethany and Mags crossed to where Jo was sitting with Lynn, Carla and a few other women. They all had that look—glamorous, exciting. Definitely not from Sweetwater, thought Bethany. It wasn't even so much how they looked, she realized. It was more an attitude that shimmered around them like heat off the pavement during a Sweetwater summer.

She plopped onto the sofa beside Jo, pulling Mags with her. Then she introduced her friend to the pilots. There was a chorus of hellos, which Mags returned in kind.

"The whole town is talking about you," she told the women. Bethany delivered a quick elbow nudge to Mag's ribs, but it was too late.

"Oh yeah? And just what are they saying 'bout little old us?" asked Carla, deliberately exaggerating her southern drawl so that "saying" sounded like "sane" and "old" sounded like "owl."

"Well...," said Mags.

"Um...," said Bethany.

The pilots sitting around them burst out laughing.

"Let me guess," said a WASP Bethany hadn't met. "They think we delicate dishes of femininity can't handle those big bad airplanes, right?"

Another said, "I bet they think we should stick to the typing pool."

Carla, who had worked at an aircraft factory, said, "They think it's okay for us to build planes, but they don't think we should fly them."

Bethany and Mags didn't know what to say. People *had* said all those things. But the WASP pilots did not seem offended in the least. They laughed as they threw out other suggestions. Mags and Bethany ended up laughing with them.

Then Bethany remembered Mr. McBeath. She told the pilots what the newspaperman had said in her father's barbershop.

A voice suddenly barked from behind Bethany, Jo, and Mags.

"Girls, it doesn't matter what anyone says. It doesn't matter what anyone thinks. We *are* going to fly those planes!"

Mags and Bethany jumped. The pilots sitting with them scrambled to their feet and fell silent. It was the reverent kind of silence you find in church, thought Bethany, not the scary you're-gonna-get-in-trouble silence or the sad funeral kind of silence.

The speaker walked around the end of the couch and joined the group. She said, "At ease, ladies, at ease," as she settled into a chair vacated by one of the pilots. Looking at Bethany and Mags, she raised one eyebrow and asked, "What have we here? New recruits?"

Nobody spoke. Bethany and Mags looked at the woman. She was red-haired, like Carla, but older. And she was definitely in charge. "Well? Cat got your tongue?" she asked.

Bethany did not know who this woman was, but she decided she wanted to know. So she introduced Maggie and herself and added, "We want to be pilots, too. Who are you? Can you help us?"

When the woman laughed, the other pilots did, too.

"Girls, I'm Jacqueline Cochran. I started the WASP."

Bethany had a thousand questions, but she knew she didn't have time to ask them. She had already stayed longer at the hotel than she intended. And she hadn't even asked Jo, Carla, and Lynn to Sunday dinner yet.

So she stood up to go and relayed her mother's invitation. She almost whooped for joy when all three said yes. Then she had an idea—an idea that would get her in big trouble, to be sure. But if it worked out, it would be worth any punishment she got.

Turning back to the WASP leader, she asked her to join the family for dinner as well.

Bethany was disappointed when the big redhead declined the invitation. She had just come to Sweetwater to take stock and get her girls settled, she said. She wouldn't be in town very long.

As they left the hotel after saying goodbye to the pilots, Mags asked Bethany *what* she had been thinking.

"It only would have been one more for dinner. Mamma would have been mad at me for not asking permission first, but she wouldn't have told her not to come," Bethany said.

"No, no, no. That's not what I'm talking about," said Mags. "I don't want to be a pilot. Why'd you say that? And since when have you wanted to be a pilot?"

Bethany blinked. She had just assumed since *she* wanted to be a pilot, Mags would too. They almost always liked the same things. Not this time, though. Mags didn't even want to ride in a plane, much less fly one.

They argued about it all the way to Mags' house, then Bethany walked the last block and a half by herself. She didn't understand how anyone could *not* be interested in flying. In her mind she again became the Purple Baroness. She was soaring through the clouds, seeking out the enemy. She was wearing Ravenous Red lipstick. By the time she got home a few minutes later, she had shot down three enemy planes. Rat-a-tat-tat-tat-tat-tat-tat!!! Rat-a-tat-tat-tat-tat-tat-tat-tat!!! Rat-a-tat-tat-tat-tat-tat-tat-tat!!!

7

Bethany gave the dining table one last swipe with the dust cloth then eyed it critically. She'd waited all week for this dinner, and it had to be perfect. Yep. It looked pretty good. Mamma had put the extra leaf in the table so they'd have room for three more people, and she had promised they could use the company dishes.

Bethany loved those dishes. They were creamy white with pretty pink flowers around the edges. She carefully took six plates from the hutch and set them around the table. Papa would sit at one end and Mamma at the other. Bethany decided she would sit to the left of Papa with her back to the dining room windows. She wanted Jo to sit next to her. Carla and Lynn would sit on the other side of the table facing them.

When she finished setting the table, Bethany went into the kitchen to check on dinner. Mamma had used the last of the ration coupons to get a roast. It was cooking now in the big cast-iron pot on top of the stove. Mamma lifted the heavy pot lid and carefully placed cut up potatoes around the roast. Then she adjusted the gas burner so the pot wouldn't boil over. She would add the carrots last.

"Bethany, I was thinking about having another vegetable with dinner. How about pinto beans?" Mamma asked.

She laughed at the expression on Bethany's face. She had been kidding. They were going to have peas.

Mamma did not need help in the kitchen, so Bethany went to take one last look through the house. Everything had to be perfect. She knew the dining room was okay, so she skipped it and went down the hall. There were fresh towels in the blue and white bathroom. She went on to the living room. Sun streamed through the front windows and highlighted the flowered wallpaper. The sofa and the two chintz-covered chairs, Papa's chair by the fireplace—it all looked fine. Everything was ready. Bethany couldn't wait for her guests to arrive! The mantle clock said it was only one-twenty. Jo and Carla and Lynn wouldn't be here for another forty minutes! Maybe the clock was slow. No, she had seen Papa wind it yesterday. She'd have to wait.

Bethany had wanted to wear pants, but Mamma insisted she stay in her church clothes. She was sure the pilots would be wearing slacks, but Mamma had been adamant. No slacks. If she wanted to use the company dishes she could not wear pants at the table. That was the deal. Oh well.

She climbed the stairs to her own room and flopped on the bed on top of the pale yellow bedspread. She would read until Jo and the others got here. *Anne of Green Gables*. It was one of her favorites.

The next thing she knew, the world was rocking like crazy. It was an earthquake! No, they didn't have earthquakes in Texas. Someone was shaking her.

"Bethany, wake up. Your guests are here." It was her mother.

She had fallen asleep! Bethany rolled off the bed and smoothed down the covers, then looked in the mirror to make sure her hair wasn't sticking up. She groaned. Her hair was fine, but there was a long pinkish crease down the right side of her face from the covers. There was no telling how long it would take to fade away. She'd have to go out there like this! This was not what she'd had in mind. If only her mother would let her wear pants, it wouldn't be so bad. But she knew better than to change clothes now. Mamma would be mad if she did.

When Bethany walked into the living room, she was glad she hadn't changed. Her pilot friends were all wearing stylish suits with short skirts. They looked more than ever like movie stars.

Over dinner—Mamma's roast was delicious!—Jo and Carla and Lynn told the Parkers about moving from the Bluebonnet Hotel to the barracks at Avenger Field.

"They took us out there in cattle trucks, can you believe it?" Jo said. "They just loaded us up like so many heifers and away we went!"

Male pilots were moving out as the female flyers were moving in, so there were a lot of wolf whistles aimed in the WASP's direction. Once on base, the women were split into groups of six and assigned to rooms in the barracks. Six women shared each room, and twelve shared each bathroom! Each woman got a cot, a wall locker, and a foot locker. Nothing more.

Because the WASP were divided up according to their last names, Josephine Nicholson and Carla Neely were roommates. Lynn Strickland was with five girls she'd never met until they moved in together, but she didn't seem to mind.

"They're great gals. We get along just fine," she said.

Carla helped herself to more potatoes as she told the Parkers about the clothes issued to them.

"Some uniforms!" she scoffed. "Surplus Army mechanics overalls—male mechanics. And not small males either! Mine are a size 48, 48 if you please! You could fit two of me in there."

It was the same for all of them. It seemed there wasn't a single set of coveralls smaller than a men's size 44. The women cinched in the waists with belts and rolled up the legs and sleeves. No one knew who said it first, but the women had started calling the oversized outfits "zoot suits."

"Carla, don't forget about the fancy headgear. You have to tell them about that," said Jo.

"Oh yes," Carla said. "How could I forget the turbans! Our esteemed base commander, a fellow named Urban, has decided we should all wear these little head wraps. Zoot suits and Urban's turbans—what a combination!"

Everybody laughed.

Bethany asked about the flying.

"One word. Brrrrrrrrrrrrrrrrrrrrrrrrrrrrrr!" said Jo. "I've been wiping snow off my goggles up there. I can't wait for it to warm up."

Bethany's father told Jo to be careful what she wished for. "You know, there are two seasons here in Sweetwater," he said. "Cold and hot."

In addition to learning precision flying, the WASP trainees were learning to march and drill in formation like soldiers.

"We march everywhere—march, march, march," said Jo. "We march to meals and we march to the flight line and we march to class. I swear I'll use up all my ration coupons for shoes and end up marching barefoot!"

They laughed again.

Before Jo and Carla and Lynn went back to Avenger Field that day, Mamma asked them to come back for dinner the following Sunday. Bethany was thrilled! But all the women were restricted to base for the next several weeks. They said they'd love to come back when the restriction was lifted.

8

The Parkers were not the only Sweetwater family to invite women flyers to Sunday dinner. Quite a few had hosted one or more of the WASP and hoped to have them back.

Not Mr. Baines, though. He was still against letting the women fly, and he said so to anyone who would listen. "Just because there hasn't been an accident yet doesn't mean there won't be one," he said one day in the barbershop, a month or so after Jo, Carla, and Lynn ate with the Parkers.

"Baines, the male pilots have had accidents. Why should the women be any different?" asked Bethany's father.

Bethany was curled up in a chair doing her homework and half listening to the conversation. She was paying a lot more attention to her geometry since Jo told her she would need all kinds of math to get a flying license. Pilots had to be able to calculate distances and fuel consumption. Knowing there was a real use for all those angles and numbers made it easier somehow.

Mr. Baines was saying that when the men crashed, they had the decency to do it outside the town. He seemed convinced that one of the WASP was going to dive-bomb the courthouse or the hospital.

Papa just shook his head. Mr. Baines obviously wasn't going to be convinced.

The bell on the shop door tinkled, and a tall blond man walked in. Bethany had never seen him before. Like the WASP pilots, he had the look of not being from Sweetwater. But he couldn't be a WASP, he was man!

Bethany's father must not have known him either, because he introduced himself to the newcomer and asked him to have a seat. If Papa didn't know him, he must be new in town. Papa knew everyone.

The stranger returned the greeting and said his name was Joseph Klein. He had the bluest eyes Bethany had ever seen. As he sat down he said hello to Mr. Baines and Mr. Collins, too.

"What brings you to Sweetwater, friend?" asked Papa.

"Oh, I am a mechanic at the airfield," said Mr. Klein. "I fix the planes."

He had a slight accent—not like Carla's southern drawl or the clipped tones of the English and Canadian pilots Bethany had met in town. Could he be German, she wondered? His name sounded German. Klein. Klein. What would a German be doing in America when America was fighting the Germans? What would he be doing in Sweetwater?

Bethany was dying to ask, but she didn't. It would be rude. Besides, Papa would tell Mamma and Mamma would scold. "You don't ask personal questions of strangers," she'd say. Mamma had a lot of rules. Papa said that was her job.

Instead, she asked him what he thought of the women flyers out at Avenger Field. She did not look at Papa or at Mr. Baines when she asked the question.

"They are very good pilots, very careful," he said. "Of course, I am new. I have only been there a few days."

Bethany looked at Mr. Baines out of the corner of her eye. He was scowling. Bethany looked at Papa. His eyes were crinkling like they did when he laughed, but he did not laugh. He kept a straight face.

"Bethany," he said, "why don't you go check at the post office for a letter from Andrew?" They hadn't gotten one in several weeks. It was the first time since he'd been gone that they hadn't gotten at least one letter each week from him.

Bethany left for the post office. Mr. Baines started talking again as she went out the door, but she couldn't make out his words.

There was no letter from Andrew, and Bethany was worried. Mamma and Papa were worried, too, but they tried to pretend they weren't.

"He's fighting a war far, far away," Mamma would say. "There are any number of reasons we haven't gotten a letter."

Papa would say, "At least we haven't heard from the Army. No news is good news." Bethany knew what he meant, but she thought no news was crummy. But she never said so to Papa.

9

Papa had a surprise when he got home that night.

Several men had visited the barbershop after Bethany left to talk about creating a special place in town for the women pilots.

Mr. Baines hadn't liked the idea, of course.

"At home, that's where their place is," said Papa, repeating what Mr. Baines had said. "Everyone ignored him, though, so he left in a tizzy."

Mr. Wells, Mags' father, was one of the men who wanted to talk to Papa. He owned the building that housed his drugstore, and it had an extra room with a door that opened onto the street. Mr. Wells had been using the room for storage, but he volunteered to clean it out and let the WASP use it as a gathering place for when they were in town—sort of like a bar, but with no alcohol. He wanted Papa and some of the other businessmen to help set it up.

"I think it's a swell idea," Papa said. "We're going to call it the Avengerette Club. Bethany, you'll have something to tell Jo and Lynn and Carla when they come to dinner on Sunday."

The ban had been lifted, and the pilots were allowed to visit town again. Bethany couldn't wait to see her friends again.

The day they came to dinner, Bethany told them about school—she was doing better in geometry, but she still didn't like it. And she told them about the Avengerette Club, too. But Bethany didn't want to talk. She was more interested in hearing

45

about what the Women Airforce Service Pilots were doing out at Avenger Field.

Jo said the zoot suits were not the only things at Avenger that were too big for the WASP. The seats in the planes could not be adjusted enough, so some of the women pilots had to sit on parachute packs in order to see and reach the controls. Jo had to use two.

Lynn asked Mamma about ways to keep dust under control in Sweetwater. There were regular inspections of the barracks, just like in the Army, and everything was supposed to be spic and span, neat and tidy. That meant no dust anywhere. "Nothing will stay dusted for more than ten minutes," Lynn said. "You turn your back and boom! you can't tell you ever took a dust cloth to the place."

Mamma could not help her, but she did sympathize. She had been fighting Sweetwater dust all her life.

Bethany loved hearing about everything that went on at Avenger Field. She asked Carla what her favorite part of the day was. Bethany figured it must have something to do with airplanes. It did, but what Carla said was not what Bethany was expecting.

"I love lying in bed in the morning, listening to the mechanics warm up the planes on the flight line," she said. "I don't like getting up, mind you, but I do like that sound."

By May, Jo and Carla and Lynn had become regular visitors at the Parker house.

As they all sat talking in the living room after dinner one Sunday, the pilots told Bethany and her parents that they had finally figured out an efficient way to clean the too-big zoot suits. They just jumped in the shower wearing one. "Lather up good and you clean the garment and the girl in one fell swoop," Carla said.

Jo told Papa that he had been right when he warned her to be careful what she wished for back in February. "I don't think I've ever been so hot in my life!" she said. The barracks were hot and stuffy at night, so the pilots had started dragging their Army cots outside at night to sleep. They studied in the heat, ate in the heat, marched in the heat, and slept in the heat.

Even though it was cooler outside at night, Carla said she still had a hard time sleeping, thanks to the snakes.

"One of the girls got up to go to the bathroom last month, and as she swung her feet over the edge of her cot she heard a funny buzzing sound. It took her a minute to realize it was a rattle-snake," said Carla. "But once she did she went to screaming, and I swear she scared all of us half to death. I woke up thinking the Germans must have invaded Sweetwater. But that's not as bad as what happened to Jo last week."

Jo told them she was on a solo flight when she glanced down and saw a snake in the plane. It seems the rattlers liked to sleep on the warm metal of the aircraft, and this one hadn't been scared off by the vibrations when the engine was started.

"What did you do?" Bethany asked

"Well, there wasn't much I could do," said Jo. "So I put the plane into a roll and flipped that snake right out of there!"

The Parkers were still peppering Jo with questions about the snake when a car pulled up and stopped in front of the house. Bethany saw through the front windows when Mr. Davis from the telegraph office got out. Her mother saw, too, and went pale.

The pilots didn't know what was happening, but they could tell something was wrong. Everyone fell silent as Mr. Davis walked from the curb to the front door. He knocked.

Nobody moved.

When he knocked again, Bethany's father stood up slowly, and just as slowly went to the door. Bethany rushed after him, but her mother kept her seat.

"Telegram for you, Fred," said Mr. Davis as he held out a small piece of paper. He spoke softly. He was used to delivering bad news. The telegram was from the Army. No news was good news.

"Papa, don't open it!" cried Bethany. If they didn't read it, they wouldn't know. It wouldn't be real.

When they walked back into the living room, Bethany's mother was standing by the fireplace, looking at the picture of Andrew in his flyboy uniform. She turned to look at her husband, then they sat down together on the sofa. They opened the telegram.

The women flyers glanced at each other but said nothing. Bethany was standing near the chair where Jo was sitting, and the pilot reached out and took her hand. Bethany held on tight as her parents silently read the telegram together.

Bethany's father looked up from the little tan-colored paper and started to speak, but his voice cracked. He cleared his throat and started again. "Andrew is missing in action," he said. "His plane was shot down over Europe."

10

It had been two weeks since the telegram came about Andrew. It was the longest two weeks Bethany could remember. Longer than the two weeks before Christmas every year. Longer than the last two weeks of school. They had heard nothing else. Nothing from the Army. Nothing from Andrew.

That first night, after the pilots had gone back to Avenger Field and her parents had gone to bed, Bethany crept into the attic. She made her way to the small window at the end of the room, threading her way through trunks and boxes. Somewhere up here there was a box filled with Andrew's old toys and books. He had laughed when his mother refused to throw them out. "You might want to pass them along to your own son someday," she had said. Thinking about that gave Bethany a lump in her throat.

When she got to the window, she pulled the stub of a candle and box of matches from the pocket of her bathrobe. She lit the candle and held it in front of the window until she saw an answering gleam from a block and a half away. Then she flicked her hand back and forth in front of the candle three times. Three flashes meant "Meet me by Miller's Pond." She waited until she saw one flash in return. One flash meant yes, two meant no or I can't.

Back in her room, Bethany quickly changed into pants and a short-sleeved shirt. Carrying her loafers in her hand, she crept

silently down the stairs and out the front door. Then she slipped
her feet into the loafers and hurried off to meet Mags.

They had started using the candle system to send messages
between their houses after reading *Anne of Green Gables* four years
ago. If it worked for Anne and Diana, it would work for them
too, they reasoned. And it had. They chose Miller's Pond as their
meeting place because it was nearby and because no one was
likely to see them there. Few people ever went there, and Bethany
and Mags had begun to think of it as their place.

Miller's Pond was called that because way back in the late
1800s there had been a little water-powered grain mill along the
creek leading to it. The mill was long gone, but the pond was still
there. It was a delightful place full of frogs and little fishes. A row
of trees screened the pond from the road, so it made a perfect pri-
vate place to swim during the hot summer months...and hot
spring months and hot fall months.

On clear evenings like this, the sky was reflected in the pond.
Gazing at the smooth surface as she waited for Mags to arrive,
Bethany thought she might be able to dive in and swim among
the moon and stars. Who'd need an airplane if you could do that?

Bethany heard someone coming. She was about to call out to
Mags when she saw a tall silhouette on the other side of the pond.
It was much too tall to be petite Maggie Wells. Bethany slipped
behind the trunk of a big oak tree on the banks of the pond and
peeped out from the shadows.

Whoever it was stopped by a clump of bushes, bent over, and
picked up something. Those bushes would be covered with wild
blackberries by the end of the summer, Bethany knew, but there
was no fruit on them now. As the person straightened up, moon-
light glinted on pale hair and shined on a face. It was a man.
Bethany knew she had seen him before, but where?

Of course! The barbershop! It was that fellow with the funny
accent, the one who was an airplane mechanic out at Avenger

Field. He had a German-sounding name. Something that started with a "k." King? No, that wasn't German-sounding. Klein, maybe? Bethany couldn't remember. She wondered what he was doing by Miller's Pond at night. She certainly wasn't going to ask him. He slipped whatever he had picked up into his pants pocket, then walked around the pond and disappeared into the trees.

When Mags showed up a few minutes later, Bethany forgot all about the stranger. She told her friend about Andrew, but she didn't cry. She was *determined* not to cry. Mags hugged her, then they sat with their backs against the oak tree and talked.

"Maybe he bailed out. Pilots wear parachutes, don't they?" said Mags.

Bethany knew from the movies and her WASP friends that pilots did indeed wear parachutes. Maybe Andrew *had* bailed out. "Maybe he's hurt. He could have amnesia. Maybe a beautiful girl, a farmer's daughter, found him and is nursing him back to health," said Bethany, thinking of several movies with that very plot. There had been a lot of films lately about heroic downed pilots. There always seemed to be a farmer's beautiful daughter involved somehow.

"Sure," said Mags. She had seen most of those movies, too. "And when he's well she'll smuggle him out of the country and he'll come home a hero."

After that night, Bethany refused to believe Andrew might be dead. He was just getting well somewhere, that's all. He'd come home, and there would be a parade down Main Street. The mayor would give him a medal, and his picture would be on the front page of the *Sweetwater Reporter*.

At school she heard the other kids whispering about her brother when she walked past. They said he had been shot down. They said he was dead. But they never said it to her, not after the first time. Not after she got in that fight with Claude Walker.

Claude had asked her why the Parkers didn't have a gold star in the front windows of their house. Whenever a soldier died, his mother got a gold star from the government. Claude had a gold star in his front windows. A lot of the families in Sweetwater did. Marcie Chisholm had *three*. She had six brothers, and three of them had died fighting in the war so far. That was more than any other family in town.

Bethany's family did not have a gold star because the Army said Andrew was missing in action, not dead. That's what Bethany had told stupid Claude. But he laughed and said it just wasn't official yet. "You wait an' see, you'll be gettin' that star any day now," he sneered.

Claude was a mean boy. He wore a crew cut that made the top of his head look flat, and he had big space between his front teeth that made it easy for him to spit on people. He was always saying hateful things and looking for a fight. He got more than he bargained for *that* day. Bethany smiled as she remembered the satisfying thunk! her history book made when she brought it down on top of his flat-looking head. Then she dropped the book, doubled up her fist, and punched him smack! right in the nose.

"My brother is NOT DEAD!" she yelled as blood gushed from Claude's freckled nose.

Loyal Maggie, who had heard the whole thing, kicked him in the shin for good measure. She was such a good pal!

All three of them had been sent to the principal's office. At home, Bethany had been grounded for a week. But it had been worth it. No one ever said anything else to her about Andrew being dead. And the Parkers still didn't have a gold star in their front window.

Bethany continued to check the mail every day. So far, there had been no new letter, but Bethany kept hoping. When she went into the post office, Mr. Robinson would smile kindly and look at her over the tops of his little glasses. "Nothing today, Bethany. I'm sorry," he would say.

She wanted to scream, "My brother is not dead!" like she had at Claude Walker. But she never did. As Bethany opened the post office door this time, she prepared herself for Mr. Robinson's kindly smile as he told her there was no mail today either.

"Good afternoon, Bethany. I have a letter for you today," he said.

A letter? There was a letter! "Oh Mr. Robinson, is it from Andrew? Is it? Is it?" she cried as she rushed to the counter.

"I don't know," he said. "But it is from overseas."

Bethany seized the letter and gazed at it. It just had to be from Andrew. She thanked Mr. Robinson and rushed out the door. She ran all the way to Maple Street and was out of breath when she got to the barbershop.

"A letter, Papa. There's a letter," she gasped as she banged open the door. "There's a letter from overseas. It must be from Andrew!"

11

They did not wait for dessert this time. They did not have dinner first. They didn't even take off their coats. Mamma ripped open the letter as soon as Papa handed it to her.

It was not from Andrew.

Mamma read in a shaky voice:

Dear Mr. and Mrs. Parker,

By now I am sure you have heard that Andrew is missing. I saw what happened and I felt I must write. We were flying XXXXXXXXXXXXXXXXXXXXXXXX XXXX XXXXXXX in formation when we came under heavy fire—flak from below and fighters in the air.

Your son's plane was hit, but he did manage to complete his mission. He is a fine soldier. You should be proud of him.

We all headed home, and for a while it looked as if the Brave Bethany would make it. Did you know Andrew had named his B-17 after his little sister?

Unfortunately, the plane was just too badly damaged. The crew bailed out when it became clear the plane was going to go down over XXXXXXXXXXX. My crew and I counted parachutes and watched them descend as long as we could. We know that one gunner was killed in the initial attack. We believe the rest of the crew, including

Andrew, made it safely to the ground. We thought you would like to know.

Andrew is a fine pilot and a good friend. He talked of you all often. He is in our thoughts, as are all of you.

Sincerely,

Lt. George Baker

Bethany knew it! Andrew was safe! He must be! He'd come home a hero. Everything would be okay.

Her parents did not seem very relieved, thought Bethany. Papa looked quiet and thoughtful as he sat on the sofa holding Mamma's hand. Mamma's forehead was wrinkled with worry. They must not understand, thought Bethany.

So she told them about bailing out and amnesia and the farmer's beautiful daughter. But they did not seem convinced. Her mother smiled, but Bethany could tell she didn't mean it. Mamma was still worried.

Bethany watched as her mother folded the letter and put it in her apron pocket. "It was kind of his friend to write us," she said.

Bethany knew her mother would put it with the letters from Andrew and read it over and over. Once, Bethany had taken Andrew's letters from the box where Mamma kept them in her top bureau drawer. Some of them had been folded and unfolded so many times that the paper had split apart where it was folded.

Bethany wished her parents believed her.

They'd see. Andrew was fine. He'd be coming home any time now. Maybe he'd bring the beautiful farmer's daughter home with him.

Mags didn't like that idea when they discussed it later that night at Miller's Pond. Bethany had suspected for a long time that her friend had a crush on her big brother, but Mags always denied it. The more she teased Mags about it, the madder her friend got. The madder Mags got, the more sure Bethany was that she had a crush on Andrew. Even the movie stars Mags liked best looked like Andrew—Robert Young and Jimmy Stewart.

"Don't you see, it's like that couple in *Casablanca*," Mags said. They had seen that movie five times before it left the theater. They never had agreed about it. Mags still would have left, and Bethany still would have stayed.

"Even if she loves your brother she can't go with him. She has to stay and do her part for the war effort in her own country. She has to rescue more pilots. She can't go around falling in love with every pilot she helps," said Mags.

Bethany had to admit her friend had a point.

"Well, how long do you think it will take him to get home?" she asked.

"I don't know. I guess that depends on how many bridges he blows up along the way," said Mags.

"What do you mean? What bridges?" asked Bethany.

"You know, *bridges*. Or railroads," said Mags. "No one ever just sneaks out of enemy territory without blowing something up. You know that."

Maggie was right. The pilots in all those movies always blew something up before escaping from the bad guys. There was no telling when Andrew would be home. He was very brave. He might stay extra long just to blow up more stuff.

12

Bethany told her mother about the bridges the next morning while they were weeding the garden.

"Honey, you have to understand that those are *movies*. They're not real," Mamma said.

Bethany knew that. But they had to get the stories from *somewhere*. They were probably based on true stories, she thought. But she didn't say anything else. Talking about Andrew always made Mamma cranky these days. Bethany wanted to go swimming with Mags that afternoon, and she didn't want to say anything that might make Mamma forbid her to go. She knew Andrew was okay. He was probably blowing up a bridge right this minute.

She, on the other hand, was stuck in Sweetwater weeding the stupid ol' garden. Bethany deliberately smashed a cabbage plant with her knee. She'd rather be blowing up bridges.

She imaged herself sneaking silently through the enemy countryside with a farmer's beautiful daughter. No, it would be a farmer's handsome son—one who looked like Tyrone Power. (Now *he* was Bethany's idea of a handsome movie star!)

They'd slip from shadow to shadow, evading the enemy at every turn. Bethany, the Purple Baroness, had been shot down after a terrible dogfight with the Nazi pilots. They had gotten her, but not before *she* had shot down *seven* of them. Then she bailed out and floated gently to the ground, just like Andrew had.

The farmer's handsome son was waiting for her. He had helped her hide and now he was helping her escape. But first they had to blow up a bridge. There it was! Bethany pulled a bundle of dynamite from a bag carried by the farmer's son. (Those farmers always seemed to have plenty of dynamite.) They set the charge and ran. Whammo! The dynamite exploded and orange flames licked the sky as the Purple Baroness and the farmer's handsome son ran off into the night...

"Bethany, watch what you're doing. Be sure to get the root or the weeds will just grow back," said her mother.

Bethany had just snapped off the top of a weed that was growing between two carrot plants. She threw it down in disgust. The stupid weeds grew back no matter *how* she pulled them! She bet the Purple Baroness wouldn't have to tend a garden. But *she* did.

They had never had a garden before the war. Well, her mother had grown flowers, but they had never planted vegetables before. Now everyone had a garden. They called them victory gardens.

Papa said it was their patriotic duty to grow their own food. He said it helped the war effort. Bethany didn't care. She hated working in the garden. It was hot and she got dirt under her fingernails and couldn't get it out. And it was full of bugs. You couldn't keep them or the wild rabbits from eating the plants. A victory garden was right, she thought sourly—a victory for the bugs and the bunnies.

But she didn't say anything. She wanted to go swimming.

It was two o'clock before Bethany made it to Maggie's house. At that time on a Saturday the city pool would be crowded, but they decided to go anyway. Along the way they talked about school. There were only two weeks to go until summer vacation, and they couldn't wait.

As they walked, Bethany noticed a man in front of them duck into the hardware store. There was something familiar about him. Then she remembered. It was that airplane mechanic, the one with the funny accent. She had seen him at Miller's Pond the night they found out Andrew's plane had gone down, but she had forgotten to tell Maggie.

She told her now. Mags was intrigued. "Well what did he pick up from under the bushes?" she asked.

"I told you I didn't see. It was dark and he was too far away," Bethany replied. They were passing the hardware store, so she glanced through the big plate glass window to see if she could catch a glimpse of him.

There he was, over in the corner by a barrel of nails. He was talking with Mr. Baines.

Seeing Mr. Baines made her think of the Women Airforce Service Pilots. He was still against them. No one had crashed yet, but he was convinced it was only a matter of time.

Bethany had not seen Jo or Lynn or Carla since the day they found out about Andrew. She had gotten a note from Jo. The pilot had said they were working hard to earn their WASP wings, but they hoped to see Bethany and her parents soon. She had said she hoped they had good news about Andrew soon.

When Bethany and Maggie got to the Sweetwater public pool, they went into the ladies dressing room to change into their swimsuits. Several women who had to belong to the WASP were there. They had that look. Bethany whispered as much to Mags, and Mags nodded. She knew what Bethany meant. Nobody from Sweetwater looked like that.

Bethany and Maggie went into separate booths to change their clothes. When they emerged, both girls stopped in shock. Two of the women-who-must-be-WASPs had stripped down and were changing right there in the open. And they didn't look the least bit embarrassed.

Definitely not from Sweetwater, thought Bethany.

13

When Bethany got home three hours later, her parents were sitting on the couch waiting for her. The house was dim and quiet. Bethany saw that Mamma held a piece of tan-colored paper in her hands.

"Bethany, come in and sit down. We need to talk with you," her father said.

Bethany looked from one to the other. What was wrong? They looked so grim.

"Bethany, we've had another telegram. Please come sit down," said her father.

The paper in Mama's hands! It was a telegram! No news was good news. Bethany quickly looked around. She didn't see a gold star.

Dragging her feet across the shiny hardwood floors, Bethany slowly walked into the living room. She shuffled to one of the chintz-covered chairs. It was the chair Jo had occupied that day they got the first telegram.

Bethany sat. She remembered how Jo had held her hand when they got the first telegram. Her heart was hammering in her chest. No news was good news. No news was good news. But they had another telegram They had heard from the Army.

She saw Mamma and Papa look at each other, then Mamma looked at the little paper in her hands and said, "It's from the Army."

Bethany already knew that.

"It says Andrew's plane was shot down over France," said Papa. France! There were farmers in France, farmers with beautiful daughters and handsome sons. Her brother's plane had gone down over France!

Papa was still talking. "It says Andrew bailed out safely." Safe! Andrew was safe! In France! With a farmer's beautiful daughter!

"And he was captured by the Germans," said Papa, softly. "He's alive, but he's in a POW camp."

Andrew was alive, but he wasn't safe! There was no farmer's daughter. Her brother was a prisoner of war.

14

tupid Hollywood people, thought Bethany. What did they know about it anyway? No farmer's daughter had saved her brother. If there really *were* farmer's daughters, they were probably all ugly. Stupid, stupid movies.

Bethany's parents didn't have any more information. Andrew had been captured and he was a prisoner of war. It was good news, they said. Andrew was alive. She knew what they said was true, but somehow it didn't seem like very good news.

Mamma had made beef and corn casserole (one of Bethany's favorites) for supper that night, but no one was very hungry. It was the first time Bethany could ever remember her parents not insisting she clean her plate.

Bethany pretended to go to bed, but she sneaked up to the attic and signaled Mags when she was sure her parents were asleep.

When they met at Miller's Pond, Bethany told Mags what had happened. They talked about it and decided the people in Hollywood didn't know anything. They made a pact never to see another stupid movie about a stupid pilot being shot down and rescued by a farmer's beautiful daughter (who was probably ugly anyway).

By Monday word had spread and practically everyone knew Andrew was a POW. That blonde guy with the funny accent even stopped her while she was walking to school and told her he was sorry to hear about her brother.

She had decided she was just glad that Andrew was alive.

When she saw Claude Walker in the hallway after lunch, she was ready to gloat. Her brother was alive. There would be no gold star in *her* window.

But before she could speak, Claude said, "I hear your dumb brother got himself captured. I bet he gave up without a fight. I bet he started crying, 'Please don't hurt me! Please don't hurt me!'"

Bethany was furious. So was Mags. (Bethany was her best friend, and Mags *did* have a crush on Andrew.) Before Bethany could say or do anything, her friend hauled off and punched Claude. His nose gushed blood. So Bethany had to settle for throwing her schoolbooks at him. Geometry—whack!—on his shoulder. English composition—boom!—right on the forehead! She missed with the history book.

Bethany was grounded for two weeks this time, but it definitely was worth it.

By the time the punishment ended, school was over. Bethany was free for the summer!

She and Mags spent a lot of time at Miller's Pond. They skipped rocks and chased frogs and climbed trees. On several occasions they saw that funny fellow with the accent wading in the pond or walking around the blackberry bushes. Papa had told her his name was Joseph Klein. Whenever Mr. Klein saw them, he hurried away.

When they weren't at the pond, Bethany and Mags visited the library or went swimming or went to the movies. But they honored their pact and never went to see another stupid film about pilots being shot down.

On the fourth Sunday of summer vacation, Jo came to Sunday dinner alone. She was happy because she had just successfully completed a check ride. Lynn and Carla were still preparing for theirs, so they had stayed at Avenger Field that day.

A check ride was a test of sorts, Jo told Bethany. After each phase of flight training, each of the pilots had to fly with a teacher from the Army Air Corps who graded her performance.

Over a yummy dinner of baked ham and lots of vegetables straight from the Parker's victory garden, Jo told them about her check ride. She had studied and practiced and knew she was ready. But before she even went out to the flight line, she stopped at a big fountain that the pilots called the Wishing Well and tossed in a penny for good luck. All the pilots did that before each test.

When she got to her plane, she could see that the hot summer wind was pushing tumbleweeds across the runway. She knew she'd have to watch out for those. The instructor was late, and when he finally showed up he was in a lousy mood. Jo was afraid he would take out his bad mood on her, but once they were airborne he turned out to be fairly pleasant. He had her do loops and spins and an emergency landing. There was no emergency, but she had to practice in case there ever was one.

Bethany imagined herself doing loops and spins, playing peekaboo with the clouds that floated over Sweetwater. She was the Purple Baroness, the queen of the Texas skies!

By the time Bethany started paying attention to Jo again, the story was almost over. As Jo taxied to a stop back on the ground at Avenger Field, the instructor told her she had passed the check ride. Carla and Lynn were waiting for her outside the barracks. When she got close enough for them to see her, she flashed a thumbs-up to show she had passed. With a whoop, they rushed to meet Jo, picked her up, carried her to the Wishing Well, and dumped her in!

Bethany imagined the scene then put herself in it. Jo and the Purple Baroness, splashing in the Wishing Well at Avenger Field!

As Jo was leaving later that evening, she told Bethany that she would have an afternoon free in a couple of weeks. "I really haven't had much time to explore since I've been here," she said. "All I've really seen is your house, the Avengerette Club, the train station, and the Bluebonnet Hotel. How would you feel about showing me around?"

Bethany said she would feel just dandy about that. She couldn't wait!

When the day came, Bethany wore the new dress her mother had just made for her. She was ready two hours early and sat in the living room alternately looking out the window and checking the mantle clock to make sure it was working.

Jo arrived at eleven o'clock sharp, right when she said she would. They stopped by the drugstore first and said hello to Maggie's father, then they stopped at the barbershop to say hello to Bethany's papa. Afterward, on the way to the library, Bethany pointed out the hardware store, the police station, and the movie theater. They stopped at the café for lunch (grilled cheese for Bethany, BLT for Jo) then went and sat on the courthouse lawn.

Bethany told Jo how Mr. Baines was always saying the women pilots were going to crash a plane on the town square. Jo thought that was funny.

When it got too hot to sit outside anymore, they wandered into Levy's Department Store. They tried on hats and shoes and lipstick and scarves. Bethany found an especially pretty scarf that she liked very much. It was long and white and flowing, and it reminded Bethany of the scarves pilots wore, except this one was embroidered with tiny purple flowers.

She liked it but only had enough money to buy one thing and she'd decided to buy a gift for Mags, who had to watch her little sisters and had been unable to come with them today.

Bethany chose a scarf similar to the one she liked, but with pink flowers. Mags loved pink.

When they were leaving the store, Jo handed her a package. Bethany knew what it was before she opened it. "Oh thank you!" she exclaimed as she tied the scarf with the purple flowers around her neck. "I love it!"

Then she threw her arms around Jo for a hug. She was such a good friend!

That night Mags used the candle signal to ask Bethany to meet at their place. Before she left home, Bethany tied her new white scarf around her neck. It fluttered in the warm breeze as she walked toward Miller's Pond. When she got to the big oak tree where they always met, her friend was already waiting for her. Mags was eager to hear about the rest of Jo's tour of town.

Bethany told her every detail that she could remember and Mags ooohed and ahhhed over Bethany's new scarf. Bethany figured that was the time to pull out the little tissue-wrapped package she had tucked into the waistband at the small of her back. She grinned as she handed it to Maggie. "Oh, it's just like yours! It's beautiful! I love it!" her friend said.

They agreed to wear the scarves to church on Sunday. Bethany couldn't wait. They would sit together and wear their lovely scarves. Afterward, they would have dinner at Bethany's house. Mamma had invited Jo and Maggie.

When the day finally came, Bethany was so busy admiring Maggie's scarf and imaging how good her own must look that she missed most of what the preacher said. Toward the end of the sermon, though, a droning wail made her forget the scarves. The sound grew louder and louder. It made *everyone* stop listening to the preacher. So finally, he stopped preaching.

Bethany heard someone mutter "tornado." Someone else said "air raid." Like most towns in Texas, Sweetwater had a siren that somebody triggered whenever a tornado was sighted nearby. After the war began, the town council decided the storm-warning siren would be used in case of enemy attack, too.

It seemed like everyone in the church had the same idea at the same time. They all stood up and started crowding into the center aisle, pushing toward the door at the back of the church in order to get outside and see what was happening. Was it a tornado? The skies had been clear when the church service started. Was it the Germans or the Japanese? If so, why would they be attacking Sweetwater, Texas?

By the time Bethany got outside the siren had stopped. There were no enemy troops in sight, and there was no storm. The sky was the flawless turquoise color typical of a Texas summer. However, there was single dark cloud to the west of town and it wasn't a tornado. This cloud was billowing *up*, not reaching down from sky.

"Plane crash," somebody said. "Plane crash." It echoed through the crowd. "Plane crash." The dark cloud was smoke, and it was coming from Avenger Field.

By now the crowd had swelled to fill the whole street as people came from all over to see what had happened.

"I knew it! One of those women crashed a plane! I said this would happen," cried Mr. Baines, pushing his way to the front of the crowd. "I said this would happen, but everyone ignored me."

Everyone continued to ignore him as they squinted into the noonday sun.

"Did anybody see a parachute?" asked Mr. McBeath, the newspaperman. No one had. That's when people started wondering out loud who the pilot was—or who the pilot had been. Like the Parkers, many Sweetwater residents had befriended members of the WASP. They had started the Avengerette Club in town, invited the women to church, and invited them into their homes. A buzz swept through the crowd as people wondered about the identity and the fate of the pilot.

"Jo will tell us when she comes for dinner," Bethany whispered to Mags.

They had been standing outside for twenty minutes when Bethany's father decided it was time to go home. They would have to wait to find out what happened. No matter what it was, the only thing they would get by standing there was sunstroke, he said.

When they got home, Bethany and Mags went into the kitchen to help prepare dinner. They peeled and sliced potatoes while Bethany's mother put the pot roast in the big cast-iron kettle with some onions, pepper, and a pinch of salt. The potatoes would be added later. When the kettle started to bubble on the gas stove, the girls went into the dining room to set the table.

They used the company dishes: one place each for Mr. and Mrs. Parker, one for Bethany, one for Mags, and one for Jo. Then they went to Bethany's room to wait for dinner to be ready or Jo to show up. They couldn't wait for her to see them in their scarves.

Dinner was ready by two o'clock, the time they always ate on Sundays. But Jo hadn't arrived yet so they waited. Two thirty passed, then three, and finally three thirty. No Jo and no word from Jo.

Bethany's mother said they should go ahead and eat. The roast and potatoes were a little dried out, but they still tasted good. Bethany insisted they leave an extra place setting at the table, just in case Jo arrived late. "I bet everyone was restricted to base, like when they first got here," Bethany said. "They're probably not letting anyone leave because of the crash."

Bethany did not see the look that passed between her parents.

15

Mags spent the night with Bethany, and when they still had not heard from Jo by lunchtime the next day they decided to go to the drugstore to see if there was any more news about the crash. Bethany knew she'd hear all the details from her WASP friends, but she was certain by now that they had been forbidden to leave Avenger Field.

When the girls got to the drugstore, they headed for the soda counter and ordered ice cream floats. Bethany got chocolate ice cream with root beer. Mags got strawberry with cream soda.

As the boy behind the counter scooped the ice cream, the girls each climbed on a stool in front of the long counter. They spun around and around on the stools until Mag's father shot them a stern look from the back of the store where he was filling prescriptions.

Down at the end of the counter, two men sat sipping lemonade and talking about the crash. It was definite, they said. The pilot had died, but no one knew who it was yet.

Poor Jo, thought Bethany. No wonder she hadn't come to dinner. One of her friends had died yesterday. She must be feeling terrible.

When they finished their ice cream the girls wandered to the back of the store to say hello to Mags' father and ask him if he had heard anything else about the crash.

No, he told them, he had heard only that the plane was waiting to land when it went into a spin and crashed into the ground. Yes, he replied to their question, the pilot had died. And no, he did not know who it was.

"I'm sure Jo will tell us all about it soon," said Bethany. She did not see the look that passed between Mags and Mr. Wells.

When she got home later that afternoon, Bethany helped her mother weed the garden and told her everything she had learned in town. Bethany still hated fighting the bugs and other varmints that got at the vegetables, but she had decided it was kind of neat to be able to take a few steps out the back door and grab something to eat for lunch or supper.

Her father got home about an hour after they finished with the garden. Papa must have had a hard day, thought Bethany. He was wearing his headache look.

He did not even take off his hat. He just walked through the house to the kitchen, grabbed his wife by the hand, and pulled her out the back door with him. Bethany peeked through the kitchen window and saw them standing close to one another with their heads bent forward. Bethany grinned. She had caught Mamma and Papa kissing before. That's what they must be doing, she thought. But why did Papa pull Mamma into the backyard to do it she wondered? That seemed a little odd. And why would he be kissing her if he had a headache?

She had no idea, but Bethany figured she could at least get him a powder to help his head. Maggie's father mixed them up especially for him. He kept them in the bathroom upstairs, so up she went to get one. When she came down with the medicine in her hand, both her parents were standing at the foot of the stairs.

Judging by the look on his face, his headache must be *really* bad, thought Bethany. She wondered if headaches were catching, since Mamma looked like she had one now too. Papa held out his hand to her, and she tried to give him the headache powder, but he pulled her into his arms instead and hugged her tight.

"Bethany," he said. "Your mother and I need to talk with you. We've had some bad news."

Oh no! Something must have happened to Andrew, thought Bethany. Those Germans must have done something to him. Maybe he tried to escape and got hurt. Maybe he was killed. She hated the Germans! This whole stupid war was their fault anyway.

Her father knelt down and looked up into her face. "The pilot who was killed yesterday—it was Jo."

Bethany just stared. What was Papa talking about? Jo wasn't dead. She was coming to dinner. Jo was her friend. Jo had given her a scarf. "No," she said. "No!" Bethany had intended to scream the words, but they came out as a whisper.

"No, no, no, no, no, no!"

"Bethany . . . "

"No!"

"Bethany . . . "

"No!" How could Jo be dead? Bethany remembered the black smoke billowing from the ground yesterday, and she started to cry. She closed her eyes and tried to see Josephine Nicholson's face. Pretty Jo with her dark, dark hair and cara-mel-colored eyes. Jo who wore Ravenous Red lipstick. Jo who wasn't from Sweetwater. But the only image that came to her mind was dark smoke puffing into a clear blue sky.

Bethany pulled away from her father. She realized she was still holding the headache powder in her right hand, but it was crumpled and damp now. She handed it to him anyway. Suddenly she realized her own head was pounding. She needed to get away. She had to think about this. Jo couldn't be dead.

But Bethany knew that she was.

16

Bethany lit the candle in the attic as soon as her parents went to bed, but there was no answering gleam from Maggie's house. Her friend had not seen the signal. There would be no meeting at Miller's Pond tonight. Bethany decided she would go by herself. She had cried in her room for hours after Papa told her about Jo. She had refused to eat supper. She wasn't hungry. But now she needed to get out of the house.

Back in her room, Bethany quickly dressed in pants, a short-sleeved shirt, and loafers. At the last minute she grabbed the flowing white scarf that Jo had bought for her at Levy's. She tied it around her neck then crept down the stairs and out the front door.

At the pond she gathered a pocketful of pebbles and then climbed the old oak tree. From a long branch about halfway up its trunk, Bethany tossed the pebbles into the pond and tried to make them skip across its surface. Most of them sank immediately.

Somewhere nearby an owl hooted. Down below her, something—probably a frog—splashed in the water. Bethany decided she was glad that Mags hadn't seen the signal. She liked being out here by herself. Mags would want to talk about it, and Bethany didn't feel like talking. She wondered what the Purple Baroness would do in a situation like this. Bethany understood that Jo was dead and that she, Bethany Ann Parker, couldn't do a single

73

thing to change that. But the whole situation stunk to high heaven. That was a fact for sure.

When she heard a rustling on the other side of the tree line, Bethany thought perhaps Mags *had* seen the candle but had not been able to respond right away. The person who emerged on the edge of the pond was not Maggie Wells. It was that odd Mr. Klein again! Bethany shrank back into the shadows and was very still. She did not want to talk to anyone, least of all a stranger.

Mr. Klein followed the edge of the pond around to the blackberry bushes, then he sat down. From time to time he glanced over his shoulder, and after about twenty minutes he stood up and walked back the way he had come.

Bethany stayed in the tree for an hour after he left, then she went home. She thought there was something really odd about Mr. Klein. "Who goes to Miller's Pond at night by themselves?" she said out loud, forgetting that *she* had been there by *her*self and had stayed much longer than Mr. Klein. But then she dismissed the man from her mind. She had more important things to think about.

Her brother was a POW, and her new pilot friend had just died in a terrible way—everything was out of kilter. Nothing seemed right any more.

A week later Bethany was dusting in the living room when a car pulled to the curb in front of the Parker house. Bethany was sure she had never seen the car before, but she knew the two people who got out of it. Lynn and Carla.

That's odd, thought Bethany. It's not Sunday. I wonder if Mamma invited them for dinner anyway?

Then her heart leapt! Maybe they were coming to tell her that it had all been a mistake and that Jo was okay. Jo could have been flying that plane but then bailed out when it was obvious the plane was going to crash. After all, that's what had happened with Andrew.

Maybe Jo was just hurt, not killed. She could be in the hospital right now. Maybe Jo had asked to see her!

Bethany rushed to the front door and opened it before Lynn and Carla were halfway up the front walkway. She smiled at them, but they did not smile back. Bethany frowned. If they were coming to tell her Jo was okay, shouldn't they be smiling?

Suddenly Bethany didn't want to see Lynn and Carla. She didn't want to talk to them. She didn't want to see them. But it was too late because here they were. She invited them in very formally and ushered them into the living room using her best company manners. "Won't you have a seat?" she said.

She offered them refreshments, but they declined. Bethany perched on the edge of a chair, the one Jo had always used, and waited for Lynn and Carla to tell her why they had come.

Lynn and Carla sat on the sofa. They looked at each other. Each seemed to be waiting for the other to say something. Bethany watched them but stayed silent.

Finally, Carla cleared her throat. "Bethany, we wanted to talk to you."

That was pretty obvious, Bethany thought grumpily, but she didn't say anything.

Carla glanced at Lynn again. For the first time, Bethany noticed how red and puffy Carla's eyes were. She was extra pale, too, and her freckles stood out like tiny paint splatters on her face. Bethany realized that Carla had been crying.

"Bethany, you heard about the crash? You know about Jo?" asked Lynn. Her eyes were red, too.

"She's hurt?" Bethany said hopefully.

Lynn sighed and looked down at her hands in her lap. Carla looked as if she would cry at any moment. Bethany knew that Jo was not hurt. She knew Jo wasn't in the hospital. Jo hadn't asked to see her.

"Jo died in the crash," Bethany whispered. "Mamma and Papa told me."

Carla nodded. "Lynn and I packed up her things to send home to her father in San Francisco. There's something she wanted you to have. She intended to give it to you herself before she left Sweetwater. She told us so a few weeks ago."

Lynn opened her purse and pulled out a small box. It looked like a box from a jewelry store. She held it out. For a moment, Bethany just stared at the box. It was the prettiest royal blue color. Then she slowly got up and took the box from Lynn's hand. She snapped it open.

Inside, in a nest of white satin, was a small silver pin in the shape of a pair of wings.

"Jo's father had it made for her when she first got her pilot's license years ago," said Carla.

Bethany took the little pin out of the box and held it in the palm of her hand, then she closed her fist around it.

"Thank you," she whispered past the lump in her throat.

"You're welcome," Carla whispered back.

It was only then, when she looked up, that Bethany saw her mother standing in the living room doorway with tears in her eyes. She had seen the whole thing.

Taking a deep breath, Bethany turned back to Carla and Lynn and asked if they knew what caused the crash. They did not. There had been an investigation, but no one was sure exactly what had happened.

Carla said, "I don't think we ever *will* know."

17

Lynn and Carla didn't stay long after giving Bethany the little wing pin. They had to get back to Avenger Field, but they promised to come for dinner the following Sunday.

After they left, Bethany went to her room and looked at the pin. Jo's pin. Jo had wanted her to have it. That made her cry all over again.

It wasn't fair! Jo shouldn't have crashed. Jo *wouldn't* have crashed. Jo was a great pilot. *Something* had caused that crash and Bethany wanted to know what it was. If the people at Avenger Field couldn't figure it out, maybe *she* could.

But how? Well, it was a mystery. She'd have to collect clues like Nancy Drew did in *The Quest of the Missing Map* and *The Mystery at Lilac Inn*. Those were two of Nancy's best adventures, thought Bethany. It was funny how Nancy always seemed to just stumble across the first couple of clues that helped her solve a mystery. Bethany would have to do the same. There certainly weren't any clues around here, though. She'd have to go and find them.

She'd talk to Papa first. A lot of people went to his barbershop. Papa always knew what was going on in town. Maybe he knew something that could help her.

Before she left the house, Bethany pinned the little wings on her blouse. The silver looked pretty against the white material.

A half hour later, as Bethany walked down Main Street, she saw Claude Walker ambling down the sidewalk toward her. That bully! He was probably going to say something mean about Jo. He always said something mean. At that moment, he looked up and saw her. Bethany scowled and balled her hands into fists. Much to her surprise, he crossed the street to the other side. Could that be a clue? Probably not. But it *was* funny. She'd have to stop at the drugstore and tell Mags.

Her friend was working behind the soda counter, but she wasn't busy when Bethany got to the store. So Bethany climbed on a stool and sipped the root beer Mags gave her while she told the story about Claude Walker.

As they laughed at dumb ol' Claude, Mags noticed Bethany's new pin and asked her about it. When Bethany explained, Mags reached across the counter and squeezed her friend's hand. Mags was such a good friend, thought Bethany. She always understood.

Just then Claude's mother came into the store with Mrs. Robinson, the postmaster's wife. They were talking in low voices, and Mrs. Robinson was shaking her head. This might be a clue, Bethany thought.

She slipped off the stool and walked down an aisle where toothpaste and permanent wave solution were displayed for sale. The two women were on the other side of the stacked merchandise. Bethany couldn't see them, but she could hear them.

"Such a shame," Mrs. Robinson was saying. Mrs. Robinson was very kind, like her husband.

Mrs. Walker, Claude's mother, said something about a "pretty girl." The women had lowered their voices and Bethany had to strain to catch the rest of the conversation. When she heard the words "tragic" and "crash," Bethany realized that Mrs. Robinson and Mrs. Walker were talking about Josephine Nicholson.

"They say she would have completed the program in just a few weeks," Mrs. Robinson said. Bethany hadn't realized Jo was so close to earning her WASP wings. The thought of that made her want to cry again.

The women had moved away and Bethany couldn't hear them anymore, so she went back to talk with Mags. She told her about Jo being so close to finishing the WASP program. Mags thought that was sad, too.

Maybe that was a clue. Maybe someone didn't want Jo to finish her training. But that didn't make any sense, thought Bethany.

She told Mags about looking for clues and invited her to help, but Mags couldn't. She had to work in the drugstore that day. Her father was short-handed and needed the help. Bethany could see that her friend was disappointed, so she promised to write down all the clues she found and share them. That made her friend smile again.

Bethany realized it was a good idea, too. She would need to keep track of the clues somehow. How did Nancy Drew do it? She couldn't remember. But I'm Bethany Parker, she thought, and I'll figure out my own system.

Before she left the drugstore Bethany bought a Big Chief tablet and a pencil. Maggie's father sharpened the pencil for her. Flipping to the first page of the writing tablet, Bethany printed her name in big block letters. Below that she added the date. She stared at the page for a moment. Then, on the third line, she wrote, SECRETS IN THE SKY—THE MYSTERY OF WHY JOSEPHINE NICHOLSON'S PLANE CRASHED AT AVENGER FIELD IN SWEETWATER, TEXAS.

18

Bethany closed the tablet and tucked the pencil behind her right ear. Then she said goodbye to Mags and Mr. Wells and left the drugstore. She stayed alert for clues as she walked toward the barbershop. Then she remembered she already had one.

She stopped right where she was and stood there in front of the hardware store as she quickly flipped to the second page of her writing tablet. Taking the pencil from behind her ear, she carefully wrote down everything she remembered hearing Mrs. Robinson and Mrs. Walker say in the drugstore. There, her first clue. She'd look—and listen—at the barbershop for more.

When Bethany turned onto Maple Street she thought about how no one had ever told her why the street had that name. That could be her second mystery, she decided—THE MYSTERY OF THE MISSING MAPLE TREES.

Papa was giving an Army haircut to Young Jake Williams when she got to the barbershop. The boy's father was there, too. He was sitting in one of the spare chairs and talking with Papa as Papa used his clippers on Young Jake. Everyone in Sweetwater called the Williams boy Young Jake. He had been named Jacob Robert Williams Jr., after his father, and his parents had intended to call him Robert or Bobby. They did for a while, but that all changed when the boy was three years old. Bethany had heard the story many times. Mr. Williams brought his son to Bethany's father for his first haircut, and when Papa was done he had lifted the child out of the chair and said, "There you go, young Jake. All done." The shop was full at the time, and the name stuck. From then on the boy was Young Jake. Now he had joined the Army and Papa was cutting his hair one last time before Young Jake left for training. Mr. Williams said it was only fitting. Bethany wondered if he'd be called Young Jake in the Army.

She was only half listening to the conversation when Mr. Williams started talking about Jo. That made Bethany pay attention. She opened her Big Chief tablet.

"The Army wouldn't pay to send her home for a decent burial," Mr. Williams said. "The Civil Service wouldn't pay either. Now ain't that a darn shame? She's out here like a good American trying to do her patriotic duty, and her own government won't even treat her right."

Bethany's father agreed that it *was* a darn shame.

Bethany wondered if this meant that Jo would be buried in Sweetwater. She imagined visiting her friend's grave with flowers—violets or lilacs or irises. Purple flowers from the Purple Baroness, paying tribute to a fallen comrade. She would wear the scarf Jo had given her, and the little silver wings, too. But she soon found out that was not to be.

"Them girls she flew with, they took up a collection to send her home to her father. Now they oughtn't have had to do that," said Mr. Williams. "If you ask me, it's a darn shame."

Papa agreed that, too, was a darn shame.

Bethany didn't know if this was a clue, but she wrote it down on a fresh page in her notebook just in case. She could always erase it or cross it out if it turned out to be a dud—a red herring, as Nancy Drew would call it.

Why red, Bethany wondered? Red herrings, Red Baron, the Red Cross . . . even *The Scarlet Letter*. Bethany counted the last one since scarlet was just a fancy word for red. Purple was a much

nicer color, she thought. If it was up to her, she'd change all the
reds to purples.

"There you go, Young Jake. You're all done," said Bethany's
father as he used the little handheld broom to sweep hair clip-
pings from the boy's shoulders. Papa said that every time he gave
Young Jake a haircut. It was their routine, their little joke.

Then he shook the young man's hand and wished him luck.
Bethany said goodbye, too. It would be a long time before she
saw him again, if she ever saw him again. You never knew these
days. Bethany was thinking of Jo and Andrew, silver wings and
gold stars.

It was noontime and no one else was waiting for a haircut, so
Bethany's father invited her to eat lunch with him at the café. He
closed up shop and took her hand as they walked the four blocks
to Muriel's.

There was no one called Muriel there now. There never had
been. The man who owned the café named it after his mother, but
she had never even lived in Sweetwater. She was from back East
somewhere. Bethany thought the café ought to be named after
someone who at least lived in Texas. The two regular waitresses
were named Dorothy and Janet, but Dorothy went by Dot. They
had worked there as long as Bethany could remember. She
thought Dot's would make a fine name for a café—better than
Muriel's.

Dot called a greeting when the Parkers walked in and took
the table in the front window. Papa knew it was Bethany's favorite spot in the restaurant. She liked being able to see the people
passing in the street, and she liked for them to see her eating with
her father.

"Well it's Papa Parker and the little Parkerette," said Dot
when she came to take their order. That's what she always said.
"Will y'all be having the usual today?" They said they would.

Papa always had a ham on rye when they ate at Muriel's. Bethany always got a grilled cheese. While they waited for their sandwiches, Papa asked about Bethany's notebook. She thought he might laugh at her when she told him she was looking for clues to why Jo's plane crashed. But he didn't.

Instead, he said, "Sweetheart, sometimes accidents just happen and we never find out why. I think this is one of those times. The crash was a terrible thing, but there's no one to blame. I think you should try to accept that."

He didn't laugh, but he didn't think she could do it, either. Grownups never believed kids about this kind of stuff. Well she'd show him. She *would* find out what caused the crash.

19

After lunch they walked back to the barbershop hand in hand. Bethany's father said he would trim her bangs when they got back if there was no one waiting for a haircut. Bethany wouldn't let anybody but Papa cut her hair. When she'd turned twelve last year, Mamma had said she was becoming a young lady and offered to take her to the beauty parlor. But Bethany refused. No matter how many times her mother offered, Bethany wouldn't go to the Cut 'n' Curl. She didn't care how old she got. As far as she was concerned, Papa and only Papa would cut her hair. Ever.

There was no one waiting when they got back, so Bethany climbed into the barber chair. She giggled when Papa pumped the foot pedal to raise the chair. Up, up, up she went! Papa fastened the smock around her neck and squirted her hair with water from a spray bottle. Then he combed through her bangs and started trimming. Snip, snip, snip. Bethany blew at the tiny little bits of cut hair that tickled her nose.

When he was done, Papa brushed her off and asked for her opinion. She gazed at her reflection in the big mirror on the wall in front of the barber chair. The mirror took up almost the whole wall. Her bangs looked fine. They were nice and even like always. That's why she only wanted Papa to cut them. Behind her she could see the snake poster reflected in the mirror. Bright red blood dripped from its fangs. The words were backwards in the mirror, but she knew what they said—LESS DANGEROUS THAN CARELESS TALK.

And suddenly she knew. She *knew* what had made Jo's plane crash!

Bethany wiggled with impatience while Papa removed the smock and let the chair down. She went straight to her Big Chief tablet and started scribbling on a clean page.

LESS DANGEROUS THAN CARELESS TALK

LOOSE LIPS MIGHT SINK SHIPS

Except in this case it wasn't a ship, it was an airplane. *Jo's* airplane. Someone must have sabotaged it! And who sabotaged things except spies? Papa had said you never knew what would help the bad guys during a war. He had said a spy could be anyone anywhere. It was so obvious! It was the Germans! The Germans had shot down Andrew's plane, and a German spy had sabotaged Jo's plane! But who in Sweetwater was spying for the Germans?

That's what Bethany would have to figure out.

First, she would need a list of suspects. She flipped to a new page in the tablet. Mr. Robinson the postmaster? No, she had already ruled him out. He was kind and his son had been killed fighting in the war. He wouldn't be a spy for the people who killed his kid. Bethany thought about that for a minute, then ruled out everyone whose kid had died in the war. She also ruled out everyone who had a son fighting in the war now. That eliminated a lot of people: Mr. and Mrs. Walker and stupid Claude, Mr. and Mrs. Collins and the Petrie family, the Chisholms of course . . . it was a long list. After a half hour, Bethany was still writing. Maybe it would be easier to make a list of people who *didn't* have a son fighting or killed in the war, she thought.

Well who would that leave? The first person who came to mind was Mr. Wells. He had no sons at all, just Mags and her four little sisters. But Bethany couldn't imagine her best friend's father blowing things up and spying on people. No, Mr. Wells was not a suspect. There was Mr. Davis from the telegram office and Mr. Wolfson, the butcher. Bethany wrote down their names. She was getting a cramp in her hand.

As she wiggled her fingers to make it go away, she glanced up and saw Mr. Baines walk past the barbershop. Mr. Baines! Of course! He had been against the women pilots from the very beginning and everybody knew it. He got mad when people didn't agree with him. He kept saying that one of the women was going to crash—and one finally did! Bethany couldn't believe she hadn't thought of him sooner. She wondered where he was going in such a hurry. Well, there was only one way to find out. She'd have to follow him.

20

Bethany tucked her pencil behind her ear and her tablet under her arm then called goodbye to her father as she opened the barbershop door just a tiny little bit and slipped out. Spy-catchers had to be stealthy, she thought.

Mr. Baines was walking down Maple Street toward Main. Bethany hurried after him as fast as she dared. She didn't want him to know she was on to him. When she got to the corner she turned left and saw him crossing the street to the Bluebonnet Hotel. He disappeared through its big double doors. Now that's suspicious, she thought. Why would someone who has a house here go to a hotel? He must be meeting a spy contact! Bethany had forgotten that *she* had visited that very same hotel *twice* when the women pilots first came to town, and she certainly had a house in Sweetwater.

No, Bethany was convinced now that Mr. Baines was a spy. She opened her notepad and wrote MR. BAINES—hates women pilots, Bluebonnet Hotel. Then she followed him across the street. But when she got inside, she didn't see him. He had simply disappeared. It was frustrating but more proof that he was a spy. Under his name on her tablet she wrote "disappears easily." Then she went back outside.

It was getting late in the afternoon and Bethany knew she ought to go home, so she headed back down Main Street. She glanced in shop windows as she passed, looking for clues. She

was getting good at this, she thought. Nancy Drew had nothing on Bethany Parker!

When she passed the hardware store, she remembered seeing Mr. Baines in there one time. Of course, he was a plumber so he was probably there a lot. But this was something different...

It wasn't until later that night that Bethany remembered what it was. She was stretched out in bed reading a new Nancy Drew mystery, *The Clue in the Jewel Box,* when it hit her. She had seen Mr. Baines in the hardware store talking with that funny-sounding Mr. Klein not long before the crash. *And Mr. Klein was an airplane mechanic at Avenger Field!* Plus, he had that German-sounding name and he made all those suspicious trips out to Miller's Pond. Mr. Klein must have sabotaged Jo's plane, and Mr. Baines must have given the order!

Bethany was embarrassed. She would make a lousy detective. Nancy Drew would have figured this one out a long time ago.

She had to tell Mamma and Papa. Someone else might be in danger—maybe Lynn or Carla!

She went downstairs, taking her detective notebook with her. It was only eight o'clock, and her parents were in the living room together. Her mother was sewing, and her father was reading the *Sweetwater Reporter*.

"Mamma, Papa, can I talk with you?" she asked. "It's really important—a matter of life and death!"

Papa looked over the tops of his reading glasses at her. He looked a little like the postmaster when he did that. "A matter of life and death is it? Well then by all means come in and sit down!"

He was making fun of her. She'd have to convince him. She'd have to convince them both. Luckily, that wouldn't be hard with the evidence she had gathered. So Bethany told them it was about Jo's crash, and she explained about Mr. Baines and how he had always hated the idea of women flying airplanes. And she told them how he disappeared into the hotel and how he had met with Mr. Klein, who was an airplane mechanic at Avenger Field. The only thing she left out was the part about Mr. Klein's nighttime visits to Miller's Pond. She couldn't tell them about that without getting into trouble, because *she* wasn't supposed to be out there at night either.

When she finished her story, she waited for Mamma to tell her how clever she was or for Papa to get up and call the police. But they just sat there looking at her for a minute, then they looked at each other.

"Sweetie, come over here and sit with us," her father said as he joined her mother on the sofa.

When she did, Papa put his arm around her shoulders and Mama picked up one of her hands and held it tightly. "Bethany, sweetheart, we know you've been worried about Andrew and we know you're very sad about Jo. Her crash was a terrible, terrible accident," said Papa. "But is *was* an accident."

They didn't believe her!

Mamma was speaking now. "Sometimes when bad things happen, we try to find someone to blame and we lash out," she said. "But the Germans who captured your brother are far away in Europe, and there are no spies in Sweetwater. What is there to spy on? Mr. Baines is probably doing some plumbing work at the hotel. It isn't right to accuse poor Mr. Baines and Mr. Klein because you feel bad. There's nothing wrong with being sad or even angry about what's happened to your brother and your friend. But it is wrong to make up lies about innocent people."

Mamma and Papa didn't believe her! Lynn and Carla were in danger, and her parents didn't believe her. She tried arguing with them, but they wouldn't listen anymore. Papa even took away her detective notebook. Then he told her to go to bed.

They didn't believe her *and* they were sending her to bed early! Well she'd show them—she'd get proof!

Bethany pretended to be asleep when her parents checked on her before they went to bed that night. When she was pretty sure they wouldn't hear her, she got up and quickly dressed. She wouldn't wear Jo's pin. She didn't want to lose it. But she did don the scarf Jo had given her.

Carrying her loafers, she tiptoed down the stairs, through the kitchen, and out the back door. She put on her shoes before starting across the backyard. As Bethany skirted the garden she startled two cottontails that had been munching on some

cucumber plants. Bethany watched as they bounded away into the darkness. There's another victory for the bunnies, she thought.

She eased her bicycle from its rack by the garage door and walked it down the grass that edged the gravel driveway. Her parents probably wouldn't hear the tires crunch on the gravel, but she wasn't taking any chances. Bethany walked all the way to the corner before she swung her leg over the bicycle's saddle and found the pedals with her feet.

She wasn't going to Miller's Pond this time. She was headed west. If her parents didn't believe her, then she'd find something to prove she was right about Mr. Baines and Mr. Klein. She was going to Avenger Field.

She had to zigzag through town to get to the road that would take her to the airfield, and that took longer than she had expected. Bethany didn't have a watch, but it *felt* late. If she wanted to get there and back before morning, she was going to have to pedal faster. Bethany had seen fancy bicycles with more than one gear in department store catalogues, but she had never wanted one. Sweetwater was flat. You didn't need more than one gear.

Bethany could feel sweat trickling down the back of her neck and down her sides. It was hot. There was a breeze, but it was too warm to cool her down very much. She let go of the handlebars and kept riding with her arms held straight up in the air. When Bethany rode like that she could imagine she was flying. The breeze did not cool her, but it did catch her scarf and make it stream out behind her.

Here she was, the Purple Baroness, on her way to foil a dastardly deed. She swooped low over the Texas countryside, scanning for any sign of the enemy agents. They had killed one pilot and were bound to kill again. But they were clever. What better place to be a spy than somewhere you were not expected?

And everyone said there was nothing to spy on in Sweetwater. No one but the Purple Baroness suspected them. It was up to her to stop them.

Bethany could see it all now. She'd find the proof she needed. But she wouldn't show it to Mamma or Papa. Oh no, they'd had their chance! She'd go straight to Mr. McBeath at the newspaper and show *him* her proof. Then he'd have a reporter write a story about the spies and about how it was Bethany Parker who had exposed them. She'd get her picture on the front page. It was a good thing Papa had just trimmed her bangs.

A loud buzzing snapped her out of her daydream. Could you have a daydream at night, she wondered?

The sound was just ahead and it was intensifying. Like anyone who had been born and raised in Sweetwater, Texas, Bethany recognized it immediately. Rattlesnake. She shouldn't be surprised, she thought. She knew the roads were warmer than the ground at night, and she knew that the warmth attracted snakes. But what was she going to do about it now? The moon was just a tiny sliver and didn't give off much light tonight. She could hear the snake, but she couldn't see it.

She decided it would be best to speed up and try to coast past the noisy serpent. With her hands back where they belonged, she gave the pedals two quick hard turns, then lifted both feet and rested them between her hands on the handlebars.

And none too soon.

The snake struck from the left, streaking out of the darkness so fast that all she saw was the faint blur of its light-colored underside. The bike wobbled, but didn't fall, and Bethany left the snake behind.

The rattling stopped, but it was replaced by a terrible hissing. What was it? She knew rattlesnakes didn't make that sound . . . but a punctured bike tire did. She realized the snake had missed her legs but caught the back tire. And the tire was quickly going flat.

What was she going to do now? Well, she reasoned, she had come this far. She might as well go on. It couldn't be very much further to the airfield. But first she had to arm herself. There might be more snakes ahead, and she'd be walking now.

Bethany peered at the side of the road and she didn't see anything resembling a snake. But to be safe, she took off her left loafer and tossed it into the area she'd scanned. Nothing. That was as safe as it was going to get. She hobbled over and retrieved her shoe and quickly stuffed her pockets full of small rocks. Then she walked on toward Avenger Field.

Keeping to the middle of the road, she guided her injured bike with one hand and tossed rocks out ahead of herself with the other. If another snake was lurking there, the rocks would either scare it away or make it sit up and rattle. Whenever she ran out of rocks she repeated the shoe toss maneuver.

By Bethany's count, she'd chunked seventy-six rocks when she realized there was something bigger ahead than a snake. There were dark blotches all along the horizon. She must be nearing the airfield.

She knew she couldn't just stroll up and ask to see the spy, please. But she had not quite worked out yet what she *was* going to do. For now, she'd keep walking. There would probably be guards—and she doubted there was a back door—so she'd have to have a good story ready. "My sister is a WASP and our mother is very sick and sent me to relay her dying wish..." Nah, that sounded stupid. Maybe she could say she was lost. That's it. She'd keep it simple. She'd say she was lost.

With every step Bethany expected to be challenged, especially since she was still tossing rocks. Now she could see a sign of some sort arching over the road in front of a small, flat-roofed building. But still, no one challenged her. When she was standing right under the sign, she realized no one would. There was no one there. The building was empty.

She squinted to see what was on the sign. It was a picture of some kind of winged girl in an aviator's cap perched on a globe. The lettering below her spelled out AVIATION ENTERPRISES LTD. This must be the place, she thought. Now what?

She leaned her bicycle against the little building. There was a gate and a barbed-wire fence behind it. After refilling her pockets with rocks and taking one last look back the way she came, Bethany stepped up to the gate and climbed over it.

Now to find her proof. She didn't know what she was looking for, but she figured she'd know it when she saw it. Since Mr. Klein was a mechanic, he probably did his sabotaging inside the airplane hangers. That would be a good place to start.

In the distance she could see a square building on stilts. That was probably the control tower. The hangers wouldn't be there. Bethany decided to check out a big clump of buildings to her right.

She approached the buildings slowly, still throwing rocks every now and then.

"Hey, what's the big idea? Who's throwing rocks? That's not funny!"

Bethany almost screamed. The voice came from less than five feet away. She was sure she'd been discovered. But no one came running. She held her breath and stood perfectly still for a few minutes. Then she sssslllooowwwwly took one step...and another. She eased forward until she could see a row of cots between two long low buildings. People were sleeping on the cots! Now she remembered—Jo had told her the pilots dragged their cots outside at night because it was too hot to sleep inside. These were the barracks, not the airplane hangars.

She backed away from the sleeping women and eased around a corner of the building. When she turned around she saw a big round fountain with stone walls. That must be the Wishing Well where Lynn and Carla has tossed Jo! Bethany wished she could jump in and cool off.

By now she was hot and sweaty and absolutely dying of thirst. She was tired, too. Though she had no idea what time it was, she knew morning couldn't be too far away. She had to keep moving. She had to find that proof.

Bethany saw another row of buildings and headed in their direction. As she got closer she could see they had rounded tops. These must be the aircraft hangars where Mr. Klein practiced his sabotage! She was so excited she almost ran the last few yards, but instead she made herself walk slowly and quietly. She tried the door of first one and then another, but they were locked.

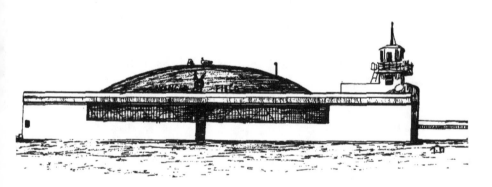

Circling around, she could see a window that was partially open. It was a bit high off the ground, but she thought she could probably squeeze through. Placing her hands on the sill, Bethany jumped and managed to get her head and shoulders into the opening. As she squirmed and wiggled to get the rest of her body through the window, she felt her right sleeve catch on something and tear, but then she was through and falling head-first to the ground inside. She was here! All she had to do now was find her proof and get off the base before sunrise. She was really tired, but she knew she couldn't stop.

Bethany searched for what seemed like a long time. There was an open-cockpit airplane inside the hangar. Someone must be fixing it, she thought—or sabotaging it! There were tools and toolboxes and what looked like cartons of airplane parts. A few canvas tarps were piled in a corner behind one big box.

She guessed that any of the tools could be used to break an airplane. Should she just take some tools and leave? She wasn't sure, so she sat down on the tarps to consider her options.

21

The next thing Bethany knew, someone was shaking her. Her eyes popped open. She didn't know where she was. What was going on, she wondered?

Then she remembered. She was at the airfield. She must have fallen asleep. Pale early-morning light filled the hangar. She couldn't believe it. She'd been caught!

Someone was speaking to her. Bethany gasped when she looked up to see who it was. It was *him—Mr. Klein, the spy!* He was looming over her with a wrench in his right hand. He must know she suspected him! He was going to try and keep her from telling!

She scrambled to her feet and backed into the corner. The hangar wall was on one side, the big box was on the other, and Mr. Klein-the-spy was in front of her. She was trapped! Then the spy stepped toward her!

With a screech worthy of an opera singer, Bethany reached into her pocket and pulled out a handful of rocks. One by one, she threw them at the spy. Thwack! Thwack! Thwack! Thwack Thwack! Thwack Thwack! Thwack!

He raised an arm to protect his face and backed away from her. She followed, still screaming and throwing rocks. By now she was mad as well as scared. When the spy turned around and ran from the aircraft hangar, she followed him.

All the noise so early in the morning had attracted a crowd of pilots, cooks, technicians, and teachers. The sight they beheld was a comical one.

One of the aircraft mechanics, a tall, broad-shouldered blonde fellow, ran from one of the hangars chased by a small grimy girl who was yelling her lungs out. The child was pelting the man with rocks as they ran. The mechanic was bleeding from several cuts on his face caused, presumably, by a few direct hits scored by the girl.

Both of them stopped when they saw they had an audience. The mechanic stood panting and dabbing at his forehead with a handkerchief. The girl stopped lobbing rocks but kept screaming.

"Spy! Killer! Murderer! Spy! Murderer! Nazi! Killer! Spy! Spy! Spy!"

The base commander pushed his way through the crowd. "WHAT is going on here?!" he bellowed.

"I don't know, sir," said Mr. Klein. "Truly I don't. I found this girl curled up in a corner of the hangar sleeping this morning when I got to work. When I woke her, she went berserk and started throwing rocks!"

"Liar!" said Bethany, still gasping from fear and from running. "He's a spy! He works with Mr. Baines! They killed Jo!"

"Bethany? Bethany Parker, is that you?" asked a voice from the crowd.

Carla pushed her way to where the odd threesome stood. Lynn was right behind her.

"Do you know this urchin, Miss Neely?" asked the commander.

Bethany started to answer for herself, but Carla told her to hush.

"Yes sir, I know her and her parents. She's a friend of mine," said Carla. "Her name is Bethany Parker, and she lives in

Sweetwater." In a softer voice she added, "She was very close to Josephine Nicholson, sir."

The commander turned to the mechanic, who was still bleeding from a cut over his eye. "And do you know her, too, Mr. Klein?"

"Yes sir, I have met her. I believe she is the barber's daughter," he said. Then he turned to Bethany. "Why did you throw rocks at me?"

Bethany ignored him. She didn't speak to spies.

"Well, child?" barked the commander. "Are you the barber's daughter?"

Bethany gulped and nodded.

"Well then," said the commander, "let's go phone the barber!"

They went to his office—all five of them, Lynn and Carla included. Bethany was thrilled. She was *finally* going to get a chance to tell her story.

But before he would listen to word from her, the commander insisted that Bethany call her father and tell him where she was. Her parents hadn't even realized she was gone. When they found out that she was, not to mention *where* she was, they were *not* happy. Her father said he'd be right out to get her, then he asked to speak with the base commander.

When the commander hung up the phone, he turned to Bethany.

"Now, young lady," he said, "why don't you tell us what this is all about? Why are you sneaking onto my base and attacking my mechanics with stones?"

Finally!

So she told them. She told them about Mr. Baines, who hated women pilots and disappeared into the Bluebonnet Hotel and talked with Mr. Klein in the hardware store. She told them about Mr. Klein's nighttime visits to Miller's Pond.

"And he's a mechanic so he can break the planes and he's German—he has an accent!" she said. Bethany had been talking so fast that she was out of breath.

She expected the commander to get up and arrest the spy/mechanic, but he started laughing instead. So did Mr. Klein! When she looked at Carla and Lynn, she saw that they had their hands over their mouths. They were laughing too.

Everyone was laughing at her! Maybe they were *all* spies. Maybe they were laughing because they had caught her!

"Bethany," said the spy/mechanic, "I am not German, and I am not a spy."

Right, like he'd admit it, thought Bethany. Papa said they didn't wear signs.

"I am Dutch, my parents are Dutch, but I was born in this country, in Pennsylvania," he said. "I don't remember talking with your Mr. Baines in the hardware store, but I have visited the pond you talk about. I like it because it is quiet and peaceful. Why do *you* go there?"

For the first time, Bethany began to think she might have made a mistake.

"But you fix planes," she said. "So you must know how to break them, too."

"I guess I do," he admitted. "But I would never do that. I did not kill your friend."

The base commander told Bethany that Mr. Klein hadn't even worked the day Jo crashed or for two weeks before that. "He was in the infirmary recovering from the measles."

Bethany hung her head. She felt miserable. She had been *so sure* she was right.

Just then her father arrived and they had to go through the whole thing again. By the time they were finished two hours later, Bethany was mortified.

She had made a *big* mistake.

Papa nudged her as they prepared to leave. She knew what he wanted her to do.

"Mr. Klein, I'm very sorry I accused you of being a spy. I'm sorry I threw rocks at you," she said. Then she turned to the base commander. "Sir, I'm sorry I sneaked on your base. I promise I won't do it again."

Both men accepted her apology. Just before she walked out the door with her father, Mr. Klein called to her and she paused. "Bethany," he said and grinned. "You are one good shot!"

22

Bethany had been right. Mr. McBeath *did* publish a story in the newspaper about her adventure, but it certainly wasn't the one she had anticipated. Instead, it told how a girl had gotten on base and accused a mechanic of spying in cahoots with a local plumber. The story did not reveal the girl's name. But Sweetwater was a small town. Everybody knew it was her.

Most people thought it was funny. Bethany didn't. She really hated being laughed at.

She got grounded for the rest of the summer—the whole summer! And because of the rationing she couldn't buy a new tire for her bicycle.

Nothing had seemed right before—and it all seemed worse now.

Andrew was still a prisoner of war. Jo was gone. Her parents didn't trust her. And *everyone* knew what she had done.

Mamma started inviting Mr. Klein to Sunday dinner—at first to apologize and then because the Parkers really liked him. He turned out to be a very nice fellow.

Bethany couldn't say the same for Mr. Baines. He did not think the newspaper story was funny. He never accepted Bethany's apology, and he never learned to like women pilots.

Bethany thought Lynn and Carla would be mad at her, but they weren't. They understood that she was sad and angry that Jo had died, because they were too. They graduated and earned their WASP wings a few weeks after Bethany got caught at Avenger Field. The base commander let Bethany attend the ceremony, but he made her promise not to bring any rocks.

***

Six weeks after Lynn and Carla left Sweetwater to start their WASP duties, Bethany was in her room reading a book (*Caddie Woodlawn* this time. No more Nancy Drew mysteries for her, thank you!) when her mother called her downstairs.

She couldn't believe it when she saw who was sitting on a chintz-covered chair in the living room talking with Mamma. It was the big redhead she'd met at the Bluebonnet Hotel back in February before anything had gone wrong. It was Jacqueline Cochran, the founder of the Women Airforce Service Pilots.

Bethany had seen her at the ceremonies when Lynn and Carla graduated, but she had been too ashamed to try and talk with her. She was sure Mrs. Cochran had heard what she'd done.

But when Bethany walked into the living room, the woman stood up and greeted her like they were old friends.

"Hi, Bethany! How are you? I was hoping you'd like to come take a little ride with me," she said.

Bethany looked at her mother. She *was* grounded after all. But Mamma smiled and nodded. Mrs. Cochran must have cleared it with her first.

So Bethany said she'd love to go. This was Jacqueline Cochran after all!

Before they left, Mrs. Cochran said, "Carla Neely tells me you have a silver pin that belonged to Jo Nicholson. Why don't you wear that today? Oh, and wear that white scarf of yours, too."

Bethany was puzzled but went upstairs to put them on. Mrs. Cochran wasn't a woman you argued with.

Mamma kissed her and told her to enjoy herself. Then she was off with Mrs. Cochran on a mystery ride. They drove west, and Bethany soon figured out that they were on their way to Avenger Field.

More curious than ever, she asked Mrs. Cochran what was going on.

"I told you," said the redhead. "We're going for a ride." And that's all she would say on the topic.

Instead she talked about the WASP and what great work they were doing. She asked if Bethany still wanted to be a pilot. (Bethany did.) Then Mrs. Cochran asked about Jo. Bethany still didn't like talking about Jo. She was still angry. She was still sad. She still didn't understand why Jo died. And she hated that sometimes accidents just happened. She told Mrs. Cochran all that, and the woman nodded. She said she understood.

Grownups always said that, but Bethany thought Mrs. Cochran really *did* understand how she felt about Jo.

They drove through the gates at Avenger Field and almost all the way to the flight line.

"I'll tell you what," said Mrs. Cochran as she stopped the car. "Let's take a flight in Jo's honor, shall we?"

Bethany heard what the woman said, but she didn't believe it. "Fly?" she said. "Me?"

"Yes," said Mrs. Cochran. "Fly. You. And me too of course!"

"But I messed everything up!" cried Bethany. "I accused Mr. Klein of being a spy. I threw rocks at him!"

"Yes, I heard," said Mrs. Cochran. Bethany blushed. Ravenous Red, she thought.

Mrs. Cochran was still talking. "You also showed a lot of moxie and a lot of loyalty to one of my pilots. I appreciate that. So do you want to take a ride?"

She didn't have to ask again. Bethany said, "Yes, yes, yes!" and hopped out of the car.

Mrs. Cochran followed, walked to the back of the car, and opened the trunk. She pulled out two fleece-lined aviator jackets, two helmets, and two sets of goggles. Bethany's fit perfectly. Mrs. Cochran, or someone, had had them made just for her!

Then they walked to a plane that was waiting at the end of the runway. It had two open cockpits. Mr. Klein was there and grinned at her as he boosted her into the front seat and strapped her in. "You hang on tight now," he said.

Bethany promised she would. She was so excited she could barely breathe.

When all was ready, the plane started down the runway. Bethany saw a tumbleweed skitter across the plane's path. The plane picked up speed and the wind roared by and then... and then ... they were *flying!*

The nose of the plane lifted, and the only thing Bethany could see past the propeller was sky, beautiful blue sky.

They circled the airfield once, and Bethany waved at Mr. Klein. Then they were leaving Avenger Field behind. They climbed up, up, up. They were flying through the clouds.

It was okay. Everything was going to be okay.

For a few minutes—a few glorious, exhilarating minutes—she really was the Purple Baroness.

The Real Story

This book is a work of fiction, but it is set in a real time (1943, right in the middle of World War II) and in a real place (Sweetwater, a nice little town about 220 miles west of Dallas). Though *most* of the characters are made up, many of the things in *Secrets in the Sky* are true.

The Women Airforce Service Pilots

There really was a group called the Women Airforce Service Pilots (WASP, for short), and it did train at Avenger Field in Sweetwater. More than 25,000 women volunteered to become civilian pilots during World War II to free up male pilots for combat duty.

Eventually, 1,830 women were accepted into the program and 1,074 graduated and earned their wings.

The WASP was formed by Jacqueline Cochran (yes, she's in *Secrets in the Sky* and she was a real person) in late 1942. At first it was called the Women's Flying Training Detachment, and it trained in Houston. Avenger Field was a better place for training, though, and the group moved to Sweetwater in early 1943.

There was another group of women pilots, twenty-five women in all, called the Women Auxiliary Ferrying Service (WAFS, for short). A woman named Nancy Love led it. The two groups joined in April of 1943 and became known as the Women Airforce Service Pilots.

When they completed their WASP training, the women pilots were assigned to military bases all over the United States. Before the war was over, members of the WASP flew every type of airplane that the U.S. military had and did everything from ferrying planes to being test pilots.

Except for Jacqueline Cochran, none of the women pilots in *Secrets in the Sky* is a real person. But the experiences of Jo, Lynn, Carla, and the other WASP are based on the stories of women who really did belong to the group. The rattlesnakes, the dust, the zoot suits, the wishing well, the Avengerette Club, and the love of flying—all those are real.

Most of Avenger Field as the WASP knew it is gone, but the wishing well still exists. It is part of a memorial to the WASP on the campus of Texas State Technical College in Sweetwater.

Like the fictional Jo Nicholson in *Secrets in the Sky*, thirty-eight of the real women pilots did die in plane crashes, eleven of them during training. The government would not pay to send the women's bodies home for burial, so the other women pilots usually took up a collection among themselves to raise the money.

Secrets in the Sky begins and ends in 1943, but the WASP continued flying until the group was disbanded on December 20, 1944.

WASP trainees wearing zoot suits, Urban's turbans, and flight jackets congratulate Mildred Davidson Dalrymple (right, foreground). Photo courtesy The Woman's Collection, Texas Woman's University.

They were the first women ever to fly military aircraft for the United States and performed a valuable service for their country during wartime. But their actions were not officially recognized by the United States until more than thirty years later, when Congress finally passed a bill declaring the WASP were veterans of the U.S. armed forces.

The group established an archive at Texas Woman's University in Denton, Texas. Many WASP artifacts are stored there—uniforms, log books, and photographs, for instance. Many of the women who flew with the WASP donated their papers to the university, and many have given interviews that are recorded there as well.

To find out more about the WASP, visit the group's web site at www.wasp-wwii.org.

WASP founder Jacqueline Cochran was born in Pensacola, Florida. Most accounts give the year as 1910. She was orphaned, and she never graduated from high

WASP trainee Francie Meisner Park gets a leg up on her plane at Avenger Field. Photo courtesy The Woman's Collection, Texas Woman's University.

Three WASP trainees including Caro Bayley (center) and Jean Babb (right) take stock of their too-big zoot suits. Photo courtesy The Woman's Collection, Texas Woman's University.

school or attended college. But she earned her pilot's license in 1932 and by 1935 had started her own cosmetics firm. In 1934 she was the first woman to fly in the Bendix Trophy Transcontinental Race, and four years later she became the first woman to win it. During World War II she flew with a group of women pilots in England before returning to the United States to become director of the Women Airforce Service Pilots in

WASP founder Jacqueline Cockran.
Photo courtesy The Woman's Collection,
Texas Woman's University.

1942. After the war she continued to fly, and during her career she set a total of thirty-three national and international air speed records. She was the first woman to break the sound barrier. By

A group of WASP trainees prepares to toss a pal into the Wishing Well at Avenger Field. Traditionally, a WASP trainee got dunked after successfully completing a check flight. Photo courtesy The Woman's Collection, Texas Woman's University.

the time she died on August 9, 1980, she had received more than 200 awards for her feats of flying.

Three WASP trainees arrive at Avenger Field in Sweetwater, Texas. Photo courtesy The Woman's Collection, Texas Woman's University.

Katherine Stinson

The woman who inspired Jo Nicholson in *Secrets in the Sky*, Katherine Stinson, was a pioneering American pilot who was born on Valentine's Day 1891 in Fort Payne, Alabama. She discovered flying while searching for a way to earn money to pay for music schooling in Europe. In 1912 she became the fourth American woman to earn a pilot's license, after overcoming an instructor's reluctance to take on a female student. She loved flying so much that she abandoned her plans for a music career. Instead, she toured the country as the "Flying Schoolgirl." In 1913 she moved to San Antonio, Texas, where she and her family started the Stinson School of Flying. She was the first woman (and only the fourth person) to master the aerial loop-the-loop, and she was the first person of either gender to successfully add a snap roll to that maneuver. She was also one of the first people to fly an airplane at night and to perform skywriting at night. In 1917 she set a long-distance record of 610 miles by flying alone from San Diego to San Francisco, and she later broke that record with a 783-mile flight from Chicago to near New York City. She

WAFS pilot Nancy Batson Crews poses beside a P-38 she ferried in 1944. Photo courtesy The Woman's Collection, Texas Woman's University.

was the first woman commissioned as an airmail pilot. When America joined World War I, she volunteered to become a military pilot but was rejected twice because of her gender. So instead, she became an ambulance driver in Europe during the war. She contracted tuberculosis, so after the war she retired from flying and moved to Santa Fe, New Mexico, where she lived the remainder of her life. Katherine Stinson died on July 8, 1977 at the age of eighty-six.

World War II and Life in Sweetwater

Sweetwater (spelled Sweet-Water at the time) was established on the banks of a creek in the 1870s as a trading post in a dugout surrounded by a group of pioneers living in tents. The creek's waters were clean and tasted good—unlike the waters from nearby creeks, which were laced with bitter-tasting gypsum. In 1881 Nolan County was organized and Sweet-Water was chosen as the county seat. The town's name was officially changed to Sweetwater in 1918. Though Sweetwater never looked as it is described in *Secrets in the Sky*, it did have a Levy's Department Store and a Bluebonnet Hotel that hosted many of the WASP when they arrived in town. Bethany and her family, friends, and

most of the townspeople are made-up characters. One of them, however, is real. A Mr. McBeath really did own the town newspaper, which really was called the *Sweetwater Reporter*. In fact, it is still called that today, but the McBeath family does not own it anymore. Though he was real, everything Mr. McBeath does and says in *Secrets in the Sky* is not.

The town did lease its airfield to the government for one dollar per year, and the newspaper really did sponsor a contest to

The visitor center at Avenger Field as it looks today. Photo by Melinda Rice.

A close-up of the visitor center at Avenger Field, featuring the WASP mascot Fifinella, which was designed by Walt Disney. Photo by Melinda Rice.

*This statue of a WASP adorns the Wishing Well today on what is now the campus of
Texas State Technical College. The plaque reads "To the Best Women Pilots in the
World" Gen. H.H. "Hap" Arnold.* Photo by Melinda Rice.

name Avenger Field. However, the Mr. Pettigrew in *Secrets in the
Sky* who won the contest never really existed.

The characters in *Secrets in the Sky* experience many things
that were part of life for the real residents of Sweetwater in 1943.
They grew victory gardens. The government rationed items such
as gasoline, rubber, meat, and sugar. Many young men went to
fight in the war, and the military censored the letters of soldiers
like Andrew Parker. Many Sweetwater residents did befriend
the WASP. The two posters described in *Secrets in the Sky* are real
posters issued by the government during World War II.

The movies, books, songs, and entertainers mentioned in
Secrets in the Sky are all real things that a girl of Bethany's age in
1943 would have encountered. And the books are all still avail-
able today!

World War II, which began for America with the bombing of
Pearl Harbor on December 7, 1941, officially ended when Japan
announced its surrender on August 14, 1945.

Sources

The WASP Collection at Texas Woman's University, Denton, Texas (with special thanks to Nancy Marshall Durr, Dawn Letson and Ann Barton) www.twu.edu/library/womens/womansc/wasp.htm

WASP Dora Dougherty Strother of Richland Hills, Texas

WASP Marion Stegeman Hodgson of Wichita Falls, Texas

Winning My Wings by Marion Stegeman Hodgson (1996, Naval Institute Press)

WASP Mildred Davidson Dalrymple of Austin, Texas

WASP Betty Shipley of San Antonio, Texas

WASP Ruth Wheeler of Dallas, Texas

WAFS and WASP Florene Miller Watson of Borger, Texas

WAFS and WASP Barbara London of Long Beach, California

WASP Lucille Doll Wise of Aurora, Colorado

For God, Country, and the Thrill of It by Anne Noggle (1990, Texas A&M University Press)

"The Long Flight Home," by Ann Darr from *U.S. News & World Report*, Nov. 17, 1997

"Zoot Suits, Parachutes, and Wings of Silver, Too," by Sheila Henderson from *CODE ONE* a product support publication of General Dynamics Fort Worth Division, October 1988, Vol. 3 No. 3 pp. 22-27

A WASP Among Eagles by Ann Baumgartner Carl (1999, Smithsonian Institution Press)

Clipped Wings: The Rise and Fall of the Women Airforce Service Pilots by Molly Merryman (1998, New York University Press)

Women Pilots of World War II by Jean Hascall Cole (1992, University of Utah Press)

We Were WASPS by M. Winifred Wood with drawings by Dorothy Swain (1978, copyright M. Winifred Wood and Dorothy Swain Lewis)

"Memories of Other Times and Other Places," a letter to the WASP from Helan Kelly Drake

Jackie Cochran: An Autobiography by Jacqueline Cochran and Maryann B. Brinley (1987, Bantam Books)

The Stars at Noon by Jacqueline Cochran, Floyd B. Odlum (1980, Arno Press)

A Browser's Book of Texas History by Steven A. Jent (2000, Republic of Texas Press)

WASP on the Web (www.wast-wwii.org)

Half a Wing, Three Engines and a Prayer: B-17s over Germany by Brian D. O'Neill (1999, McGraw-Hill)

A Wing and a Prayer: The 'Bloody 100th' Bomb Group of the U.S. Eighth Air Force in Action over Europe in World War II by Harry H. Crosby (1999, Robson Book Ltd.)

The Casablanca Companion: The Movie Classic and Its Place in History by Richard E. Osborne (1997, Riebel-Roque Pub.)

The Star-Spangled Screen: The American World War II Film by Bernard F. Dick (1996, University Press of Kentucky)

The Second World War by John Keegan (1990, Penguin Books)

Total War by Peter Calvocoressi and Guy Wint (1972, Penguin Books)

1941: Texas Goes to War by James W. Lee (Editor), Kent A. Bowman (Editor), Laura Crow (Editor) (1991, University of North Texas Press)

America in the 40s: A Sentimental Journey with a foreword by Bill Mauldin (1998, Reader's Digest Association, Inc.)

V for Victory: America's Home Front During World War II by Stan Cohen (1991, Pictorial Histories Publishing Company)

Wartime America: The World War II Home Front (American Ways Series) by John W. Jeffries (1996, Ivan R. Dee Inc.)

Sweetwater Chamber of Commerce, P.O. Box 1148, Sweetwater, TX 79556 915-235-5488 (www.camalott.com/~sweetwater)

City-County Pioneer Museum in Sweetwater, Texas, 915-235-8547

Nancy Drew.com (www.nancydrew.com)